Dedicated to the most wonderful institution of a person's life, Family

THE LOST AFFAIR

Dr. Preeti Batra

Invincible Publishers

First published in India in 2018

ISBN: 978-93-87328-88-4

Invincible Publishers

G-120, Sushant Lok III, Sector 57, Gurgaon-122002

Registered Address: Opposite Kasturba Ashram, Radaur, Haryana - 135133

Cover Designed by: Ashish Samant

Printed at Thomson Press (India) LTD

Acknowledgement

It's a wonderful opportunity to state my acknowledgements to dear God who has been instrumental throughout in bringing out my varied expressions in the form of the characters in this sweet love story. My sincere regards to my parents' in law for being so supportive. Thanks to my parents for instilling in me the best of their value system and inculcating the 'never-say-die' attitude towards life. I am really thankful to all my near-and-dear ones who were in favour of (or against) my decision to get this work published. It's my pleasure to pay my sincere gratitude to Invincible Publishers for believing in my work. As my book says, perfection lies in overlooking imperfections, I want to thank all my prospective readers who, I am certain, can guide my writing instincts to create more and better stories.

All this, however, seems to be a dream-come-true situation, and it would not have been possible without the unfathomable support of my husband, Mr. Umesh Batra. Last, but not the least, I really admire and am grateful for my children's patience to deal with their 'mamma's new book'.

To be with you is what I want,
To live with you is what I wish
Your smiling face inebriates love in me
Your fondling fingers create depth in me
The cravings, the yearnings of being together
It is just unjust, to blame one another
Time! Oh time you played the blunder
You should be responsible for the thunder
How to blame and whom to complain
Ruthless! It is selfish to think it again
You and me was the only story
But we were fallen apart with glory
The glory of relationships left us alone
We grew apart and the young years gone.

Chapter 1

The Usual Morning

It was the usual chaotic hour of the morning and Kavita was busy in the kitchen, struggling with time, so that she could send her husband and children off on their daily routines. The lady of the house looked like an incarnation of *Ma Durga* at that moment, working tirelessly with nine pairs of hands at a time. A most dreadful thing happened unexpectedly, the mother-in-law stamped over Tanay's shoes, which lay on the floor unattended. A sudden burst of her angry voice worsened the situation.

"You are fourteen now. Start organizing your things. Back in our time, children of your age would start earning. Look, what I've made out of your father." Dadi's grumbling provoked Tanay to retaliate.

"Why don't you sit in your room or help mom in the kitchen while we get ready for school?"

No one had the time to deal with that at that moment.

Anil, Kavita's husband, steered the situation wisely by distracting Tanay to something else.

Dadi kept murmuring something to herself.

"Anil, please ask Tanvi to come out of the bathroom. It is getting late," Kavita shouted from the kitchen. Within the next two seconds, she screamed, "Tanvi...you'll miss the school bus. Finish your work quickly," without giving much time for her husband to do anything.

Their thirteen years old daughter, Tanvi, would take her own sweet time to finish her work. The teenager loved to be in her own imaginary world, her fairy-land where nobody could stop her from doing anything. Her mother's beckons broke her train of thoughts running over her rules-free-zone and brought her back to reality. She hurriedly resumed her work with a last minute bustle. While getting ready, she suddenly remembered something.

"Mamma, where is my science project file? I've to submit it today," she told Kavita.

"This is too much. It was right there at your study table. Just look around. I don't know why this girl always creates a last minute rush." Kavita went on burbling, a clear sign that she would not help Tanvi at that hour. She made a grumpy face and turned to look at her dad. As always, Anil gave in and started looking for the file quietly. When he found it, he handed it over to Tanvi and advised her to be more organized. She grinned and stuffed her file inside her bag.

The clock was ticking fast. As Kavita filled up their water bottles, while looking at the running hands of the clock simultaneously, her mind tallied through her morning checklist. Their lunch boxes were ready, Papa's tea was on the stove, Tanvi's hair was yet to be plaited, and Anil's tie was on the iron table. *I've to cut a papaya for mamma and remind Tanay to take his football with him.* Kavita's thoughts were testimony to the great skills of planning and organization that a woman possesses. Such multitasking is actually inherent in women because they are always assigned too many responsibilities together. Perhaps God made women with this special ability of holding command and handling so many things at the same time. Yet, not a single relation empathises with the women folk. The complain mode is always 'ON'. There are no perks or emoluments for the laudable jobs they do, but a single mistake by them and everything goes to nought. What a paradoxical orthodox way this is of regarding women, who only wish to get a paltry of pampering for themselves, but…

At last, everything settled down in time. Anil dropped the children at the bus stop. Everyone had their morning tea. Kavita packed Anil's lunch box. She then took a seat at the dining table for a while and looked at the clock with a victorious smile on her face, as if she had won the battle against it. She knew that she had to prepare breakfast before Anil got out of his bath, so she got up, bracing herself for the next phase of her battle. She laid the breakfast down for everyone and went back into the kitchen to make some tea. While everyone else had their breakfast, she rushed to take bath and came back to the dining table in no time. Anil was sipping his tea with the newspaper in his hands. Kavita had made toast for herself and took a seat near Anil. "I've to clear the electricity dues today. Let me rush or else, there will be a long queue there, and I can't bear to stand there for too long in such scorching heat." Her overdriven mind kept thinking about 'what's next?'. "Anil, please give me cheque for the electricity bill. I'll leave for their office in a bit."

"Relax." His pitch was a little higher than usual. "Eat your meal patiently, at least. You have got time for everything and everyone else, but me," he grumbled.

"Oh! dear, is that it? I'll just get my tea. Would you like to have something else?" she smiled.

Anil's voice melted like the wax closest to the wick of a candle when it is first lit. He realized in an instant that his wife was one of the most amazing women on earth, who had been a panoply of emotions for all her relationships. However, there was definitely a missing string amidst them. They were joined together through a chord of endless relationships, but the longitudinal measure of that chord left them longing for each other. Anil often missed the loquacious, chirpy and attractive woman he had married, all those qualities of whom had gotten eroded due to the mountain of responsibilities she had taken up with regard to her in-laws and children. To add to it, the non-cooperation between these two generations with the huge generation gap, made it even worse.

The head of the family, Jagmohan ji, Anil's father, was a smart and jovial natured person. He was a retired banker. In his quintessential kurta and pyjama, he loved to spend time with his music system. Classic old songs were his true love. He hated the new movies, especially the ones with the lewd lyrics of our modern times. Everyone in the family was aware of his staunch feelings against the new age songs, as well as his touchy attitude towards the old melodies. At times when he would get carried away with an old rhythm and singalong, Tanay would quietly hum the new songs, just out of his earshot, to avoid any kind of a clash with his favourite person on earth. Dadu talked to him about everything, though both of them had very different choices and vivid ideas. Sometimes, Kavita wondered why her father-in-law always remained in his own world. One day, Tanvi was caught singing '*munni badnaam hui*' by him. What followed was a full lecture time for the poor girl. When she entered her room later, with tears brimming her eyes, Tanay burst into laughter. " Sis, you had a tough time," he said, pulling her leg.

"Shut up, or else I'll complain about you to dadi."Everyone in the family knew that dadi and Tanay were poles apart. However, no one could rule out Dadi's predilection for Tanvi. She was her dadi's favorite. Who talks about gender inequality? Kavita deeply appreciated her mom-in-law (Krishna ji) for this. Krishna Ji always had a favoritism towards girls. During her younger years, she had worked in a school and raised her two children with utmost grace. People used to envy the way she inculcated values in her children, Anil, and her daughter Aayesha. She liked to boost about the way she had raised them. She actively participated in social activities too. She would always talk about women liberalization. Although she was not a typical mom-in-law, there were some minor issues with her. She always supported Kavita in everything but would demand supremacy in all decision-making around the house. Being the elder lady of the house, she undoubtedly deserved to be respected. Kavita always made sure to give due regard to her in-laws. After all, with a little effort made towards relationships, she enjoyed a decent environment at home.

Undoubtedly, they had everything which could make a home, sweet home, yet the usual course of life often got upset due to the mismanaged and consistent discord between the varied age groups in the house. That was the only point of concern for Kavita. It was too hard to even think about some coordination between the elder and the younger ones. She often found herself enmeshed in many such odd circumstances. On top of everything, their denial of this poor balancing found its scapegoat in her only. She tried hard at times to seek help from her husband, but it was like calling the stars to come down to earth.

Anil worked in the hospitality sector as a manager to a seven star hotel. He had given so much in his 16 years of service to the oganisation that his individualism was well distinguished in the hotel industry. The kind of salary and perks he got from his job, fetched him a decent life style; a 4-bedroom flat in a posh locality, a luxury car, a lovely wife, adorable teenage children, loving parents: What else could be the definition of a blessed life? Besides that, Anil had a great deal of respect towards his personal and professional life. His indubitable feelings towards his parents often earned him the tag of Shravan of *kalyug*.

Kavita, on the other hand, was a commerce postgraduate who pursued her teaching career after her marriage but then found herself unable to deal with her teenagers' tantrums, along with their grandparents' readjustment pattern to them. About a year ago, she decided to leave her job in the interest of her family. Women prioritize as per the circumstances and it is not always that they are forced to take certain decisions. Contrary to the usual practices in an Indian joint family, she had always enjoyed a non judgmental attitude at home, which was probably the reason why she adapted so well to her environment. As a matter of fact, if women start judging it themselves, with regard to what needs to be chosen and what not as per the requirements, no grudges would follow.

Anyway, Kavita was actually the grapnel amongst the most incompatible of age groups in her family. The tussle between them was so combustible that leaving them alone together was an invitation for disaster. However, she managed the whole household and was always tipping on her toes to keep everyone in the house happy. Her phone and her car were her lifelines. Oops! Not to be missed, another very important person of their life,'Kalki *bai*'. She had been working for them since Tanay was 4 and could not even speak Kalki's name properly. He would call her Claccy aunty. The word claccy would make everyone roll on the floor with laughter, but soon became the nerve of the house.Claccy aunty would come and settle the scattered, blemished mornings of the house. Life would resume back to normal as soon as she entered.

Overall, this was their small family, juggling together their daily routines, with an essence of love and care for each other. Pause...*was it truly the essence though?*

Chapter 2

The Missing Streak

Routines! Our lives seem to always revolve around routines. Everyone is running without any motive. We are slaves to our wants, the fulfilment of which has become the only motive of living. Economics has taught us the concept of scarcity; the wants are unlimited, but sources are limited. If it is true, then why run behind those never ending wants? However, there is no escape route.

Kavita and Anil were no exception. The monotony of routines had forced them into an estranged relationship. Or perhaps, they were going through what psychologists call the'Middle Age Crisis'. Men and women entering their 40's face an array of problems related to their bodily changes. They get emotionally weakened to handle certain situations and generally eschew from being adventurous. At this point of time, a person actually needs someone to listen to them completely and keep boosting their self esteem. This middle age crisis is often felt by all human beings. In case the husband and wife are unable to do the needful, the person starts looking for support outside of their marriage. Kavita and Anil also faced this critical setback of their tender age.

Kavita always seeked Anil's attention to explain to him the mismatch between the two generations, but Anil would always sermon her about her own behaviour towards them. Expecting a solution out of him was next to impossible. At times, she just needed someone to listen to her heart without commenting, just a shoulder to lean on or a few words of appreciation. It was not that she expected a credit for all that she did, but there was a streak missing somewhere which she could not place a finger on. Perhaps, she was unable to locate the exact locus of those irritating problems which had stolen her peace of mind. She even tried alternative routes to solve her problems, but soon realized that only God could help her. The other route was her dear father-in-law, who hardly involved himself in any kind of a debatable situation.

Kavita recalled that day she had gone to Jagmohan ji and asked him to intervene in a scuffle going on between Krishna ji and Tanay. She had actually been skeptical about his response but the way he had responded, still sent tickles up her nerves. She recalled the whole sequence again.

"Papa, it is really difficult to make Tanay understand at this age and Mama becomes so adamant when I talk to her about him. Please help me out."

While enjoying Kishore Da's incredible voice, he looked up at Kavita in a jovial mood and said, "*Ye jawaani hai diwaani*, beta. How will he understand? He is moving towards his *jawani*. As for you mama, even if Lord Krishna were to come down toEarth, he wouldn't be able to move this Krishna, the rock, from her place. You know, *samjhana bhi mushkil, batana bhi mushkil*."

It was very difficult to expect any kind of interference from him. He even kept his time as per his songs. Like, bathroom time was equal to two songs, shaving time meant four songs and breakfast was to be finished within three songs. Songs basically dictated his life management mantras. To expect him to leave his song mode was next to impossible. Yet, Kavita tried her luck, but soon understood well enough that no one could help her and that she would always remain a part of this dark well. "Oh God! Why is the law of diminishing marginal utility not applicable on old songs," she would often think.

When we are right, we are guarded and when we are wrong, we are guided. Sometimes, only this much is expected from our elders, and we too need to do the same for our children. But, what if we find ourselves to be the middle segment of the chord? The first and the last segment pull and push the middle one. When that happens, the middle segment only wishes to blast off and runaway. Kavita and Anil often felt pulled by these tightly strung ends on either side.

Anil was a very industrious and highly committed person. He was always in favour of a peaceful environment at home. Actually though, he had left all such responsibilities to his wife and would interfere the least in all matters of the house. Apparently, the generation gap had not affected him all too much, as his job hours were too long and barely gave him enough time to spend with his family. Despite his long job hours and the responsibilities that gave him work related tensions, he never carried his burden back home. As a dutiful wife, Kavita always tried to comfort him as much as she could, but Anil would always blame her for not taking good care of him.

Sometimes, Kavita cursed herself for having chosen her family over her own individual identity. At times, she would sink into her own supposed comfort zone. Housewives, they say, stay in a imaginative comfort zone, but ask a housewife once, how comfortable she is.She loses herself by dividing her identity into that of a mother, a wife, daughter-in-law, all of which roles come with endless expectations. That's not all, any deterrence in either of these roles is treated as a sign of being irresponsible.

Needless to remark, Kavita and Anil were the victims of this middle age crisis. It was this monotonous etch that needed to be broken. It's just a normal condition which often aggravates due to an increased communication gap between the couples. Here too, Anil hardly discussed things about his office at home and always refrained from discussing family issues. At the end of the day, both of them found themselves looking for a shoulder to lean on.

Our society is unwilling to accept post marital affairs, but it is with such things in life that one tries to justify any kind of deviance. Sometimes, we validate such moves with reasons, but abstain from accepting our fault due to societal pressures. It is the much awaited 'CHANGE' which is needed to intersect the monotony of out routine.

The couple in our story had been going through this difficult phase in their life but were not able to express their expectations to each other. Pushing things any further would have invited unnecessary trouble and leaving the problem as it was without treatment had started to fester and deteriorate their relationship. They were always short on time to spend with each other, as they had a long priority list to attend to first, related to so many lives attached to them. They had everything that could be needed for a happy married life, yet the effectiveness of their relationship was at stake. It was impossible not only to quit, but also to continue this way.

Chapter 3

Different Strokes

A commotion at the hotel perplexed Anil when he entered his office that morning. The management had decided to open up a training department. The area head manager of the training department had to join the office that day. Perhaps that was the reason behind the hyped environment, Anil thought. They had arranged a welcome party for the new entrant. But what was the reason for all the chaos?

His inquisitiveness was soon answered when she entered the conference hall, where all the arrangements had been made up to the mark. What a ravishing beauty she was! The lady was in her mid 30's and looked no less than a fresh muse. Anil welcomed her with a lovely bouquet. He politely asked her to say a few words to her welcome party. She accepted the offer gracefully. "Hello everyone, I am Rakshanda. I know, this is a new responsibility added to enhance the goodwill of our hotel further, and is going to increase your work load a bit, but I assure you that we can work through it together." She then paused, smiled and looked over at the hooked staff. She then spoke about ethical strengths in the hospitality industry, while the staff 's eyes were being entirely unethical. Everyone was more interested in scanning her beauty than listening to what she had to say. While the women in the audience were struck by the J-factor, the men couldn't help but admire her. Even Anil could not keep himself from being a little extra chivalrous to the lady. Who can question the natural tendency of the law of attraction towards the opposite sex? The lady also noticed the handsome, fit, active, decent and witty manager of the hotel, whose planning and organizational skills were marvellous.

However, Anil soon grew anxious with the attitude of his staff and tried to convey his annoyance through his actions. He warned his staff to maintain discipline. Within seconds, things got under control and everybody resumed their respective jobs. After the formal get together, Anil accompanied Rakshanda to her cabin.

"You are Mr..." Rakshanda initiated.

"Anil."

"I guess Mr. Majumdar did mention you. I appreciate your style of working. You have done a wonderful job and your staff is really enterprising. Kudos to your leadership tactics and the way you have added laurels to the reputation of the hotel in your city."

Who in the world would not want to get such appreciation? "Thank you, Rakshanda," Anil replied. He wanted to be at ease and comfortable with her but refrained from being too friendly with the lady. Perhaps he was trying to abstain himself from appreciating the flamboyant woman.

On the other side, at the home front,Kavita found herself confronting the never ending argument between Tanay and Krishna ji again.

"You have just come back from school. No greetings to the elders? You should learn some good manners," Dadi chided Tanay as soon as he entered the house. Tanvi, as usual, gave her a hug.

"Don't start again, dadi. I am really tired," Tanay said, visibly upset about something.

"Oh, really? How much time does it take to say a simple 'good afternoon'?

"Okay then, good afternoon!" he said rudely and fled to his room.

"Is this the way to speak to your elders? There is no respect left in this generation. How does it affect me? Their parents are going to suffer. Such a loud mouth they have for a son. Telling them anything means inviting trouble for yourself," dadi grumbled on.

Kavita served lunch onto two plates and went to their room.

"Hello kids! How was your day? What happened, Tanay? You seem to be upset. All well?" she asked the routine questions.

"We lost the tournament, Mom. I don't want to eat anything," Tanay said to his mother, grieving.

Huh, poor boy. Kavita felt really bad and understood the reason behind his salty behaviour with dadi.

"Son," she spoke calmly, "Winning a game is not the most important thing, but keeping alive the spark to win anytime is. Don't lose heart. This was not your last game, you see."

By that time, Tanvi had switched on the T.V. and since her brother was not in a good frame of mind, she enjoyed the privilege of watching her programme first.

While picking up their scattered uniforms, Kavita shared with them her thoughts on their grandparents.

"The elders of the house are like the shade of a tree. When the shade is gone, you'll feel the heat. We are your parents, and your grandparents are the parents of your parents. That should be enough reason to respect them. Please don't lose your cool with them. They are growing old, and the bearing capacity of their heart and mind is deteriorating too. Please don't offend them."

Undoubtedly, Tanay had been acquainted with the statement, but was in no mood to keep his views upfront at that time. He took his plate of food and changed the channel, causing a fight to start with his sister.

That was it for Kavita. She rushed out of the room and went to the kitchen. While arranging the utensils in the sink, she felt like screaming. No one could ever imagine her state of mind. Being a coordinator and dealing with relationships was such a difficult task! It was way easier to achieve targets at the work place, but at the home front, all targets are pointed towards the woman of the house. She aligned the kitchen and went to her room. There were other tasks lined up for her for the evening, like Tanvi's project file, Tanay's science exam, the evening snacks, preparation for dinner and what not. The list was actually endless. This seething helplessness had charred the serenity which had been her strength once upon a time. Her mobile rang just then and she gathered herself up to take the call. It was Nandita *di*.

(Nandita was Kavita's elder sister, but was more like a mother figure for her. Soon after Kavita's marriage, they had lost their mother. Since then ,Nandita *di* had been overly protective about her. Kavita was also very comfortable in talking her heart out to her. Although she was far away, social media and such technology had shrunk the world for them. Nandita was almost ten years elder to her. Her daughter's engagement ceremony was about to take place the coming week and since the groom belonged to the same city as them, she had asked Kavita to book a farm house for them for a week. It was not difficult at all as Anil's connections in the hospitality industry were good enough to manage that at short notice.)

She picked up the call.

"Di, it must be easier to run a country than this mad house, and I am so tired of doing it single handedly. I suppose, if housewives go on strike for one day, the economists will finally get to know of their productive contribution. When the 'productive factors' of the country will take care of the house, our economic parameters will get to know how their GDP will move. Just a day's strike by the housewives, and I am sure no one would dare write in economics books that the work done by housewives does not contribute to the GDP."

Her sister's guffaw from the other side put a halt to her rant. "You remind me of your college time, Kavita. This is wonderful, a nice debatable issue this is."

Kavita realized that she had scratched up a minor problem unnecessarily. She smiled and asked about the wellbeing of her family. Nandita was well aware of the problems Kavita had to face at her home. She was a real guiding factor for her and would always advise her to be more patient.

"Kavita, don't hold too much in your heart. Release it and move on. Everyday, these situations will come to laugh at you. Instead, start laughing at the situations and they won't irritate you anymore," Nandita told her.

She felt relaxed and light on hearing her sister's words. She then reconciled herself to gear up again and check the home assignments of her children.

As a matter of routine, the day proceeded and after clearing off the dinner plates, she looked at the wall clock. It struck 9:30. She went to her children's room to check if any of them needed her help.

Back to the kitchen then, she rounded up some preliminary cutting and chopping required for the next morning, to save her skin during those deadly stressful morning hours. Then, she ironed the kids' school uniforms.

The clock struck 10:30 when she finally entered her room, too tired to stay awake any longer, but she had to, to show her husband that she really cared for him.

Anil was watching the news hour on his favourite debate channel. Had it been one of those previous days when Kavita used to actively participate in those debates, it would have been tremendously interesting and fun for Anil. But these days, the only debates she was a part of, were the nonstop non-sensible ones between the younger and the elder ones in the house. The news hour on T.V. then sounded nothing more than unnecessarily howling to her on issues which they very well knew would not be affected in the least by their hue and cry. Gloomily she glanced at T.V. and then went straight to the wash room. After washing her face and applying her night cream, she climbed onto their bed.

"Anil, can we talk about certain things? It's serious." She wanted to finally talk about the growing misunderstandings in the house.

Anil was too engrossed in the ongoing debate and didn't reply to her.

She nudged him and asked again, “Can we talk?”

“Uh…yeah…what is it?” He responded in fractured monosyllables.

She never liked to chivvy him often, but at times she craved to release her pressure by sharing her problems with him. She knew that it was quite difficult to talk to him about anything at that hour, yet she got really annoyed at that point. *If not you, who else will listen to my problems?* The hooter was ringing loud in her head, but she couldn't wait for his program to finish as she had to sleep on time.Her cell phone showed only 6 hours and 30 minutes remaining before the next alarm.

By the time Anil's program got over and he looked at her, she was fast asleep. He kept looking at her for a while. He thought about the exotic aromas, the stupendous layouts, and the fancy showbiz of his workplace and contrasted it with his life at home. He could not stop comparing Kavita with Rakshanda. *How fresh she seemed and how pale Kavita looked while sleeping.* He breathed a deep sigh and reclined back inhis bed.

Why was life such a roller coaster ride with different strokes?

Chapter 4

The Engagement Ceremony

Life moved on smoothly. Everyone in the family was overtly excited about the approaching engagement ceremony. It was not easy for Kavita to arrange the outfits and accessories for everyone.

"Mamma! Let's go to *Rangrez* for your saree. We will look for a dress there for Tanvi too."

"Good idea! *Rangrez*, that new designer boutique! Sure, it has a good variety of gowns too. I think we should leave by 11. Your papa will be at home then. So we need not worry about the household work either."

Shopping is a delight for the ladies anytime and at any age. Kavita, along with Krishna ji, went to the mall to shop, while Jagmohan ji enjoyed being on his own at home. After all, who does not enjoy his own space?

Both the ladies enjoyed shopping and as it was being done for a particular occasion, it had to be specific. The duo had coffee together after buying all the required stuff and then planned to go to the boutique to give their blouse pieces for stitching. It was time for the children to come back from school, so they postponed their program till the evening. They had managed to get a beautiful dress for Tanvi too. Kavita jotted down all her market errands on a piece of paper to avoid last minute jitters. More than anything else, she had to schedule an appointment with the beauty salon for mamma and herself. Who says good management is not required to run a house? Tight schedules fetch the best results at times.

While getting her facial done, Kavita got engrossed in her own thoughts. It is quite surprising that our milieu dictates our lifestyle. We are so bound by our social adjustment patterns that finding time for ourselves is commanded by special occasions only. In a way, it is correct that we don't grace an occasion, but the occasion graces our mindset to preen ourselves. And that's the beauty of occasions.

"Didi," said Meetu (the girl who was doing the facial), interrupting her thoughts. "You've come after such a long time. Take a body spa also. It is really relaxing."

Kavita was in full mood for self indulgence so she agreed to the proposal.

It was after a long time that a family occasion was taking place. In all the excitement, the altercations at home had subsided too. Nandita *di* had already arrived the previous evening with her family and was staying at the same farm house where the function had been arranged. Everyone was too tired to meet, so they co-ordinated everything on the phone. They wanted to take as much rest as they could, for the next day was full of events. However, Anil was well acquainted with the event manager, so there was no question of any kind of mismanagement.

Finally, the engagement day arrived.

Anil got back from work at noon itself. As pre-decided, they had to reach the venue much before time. Everyone got ready on time, but Kavita took a little extra time in front of the mirror. She was the last one to start, so it was natural for her to finish last too. Anil got restless, as he had been waiting along with everyone else in the drawing room for her to arrive.

At last, he got up and went to his room to tell Kavita to hurry up. Kavita walked out of the room the same time he reached there. They collided in the doorway. For a brief moment, they shared an eye contact. He stood speechless. She was attired in a beautiful off-white saree with violet pleats, and light stone work over lavender coloured embroidery. Her well-cut blouse, the single string-ed diamond necklace and long dangling earrings made her look very graceful. Her swept-back hair, without a hint of grey in it, added even more to her beauty. The fresh facial and hair spa actually proved their worth in Anil's admiring eyes. He kept looking at her, as if enchanted. If only time could stop for a while and let him relish her beauty to the fullest! Kavita pinched him back to reality and asked him, "*Chalen*?" (Shall we leave?)

The natural attrition due to the growing age makes us vulnerable to circumstances. A little attention to oneself then naturally brings out stupendous results.

They reached the venue as scheduled. The cousins ensconced together after a long time. Krishna ji got busy in looking after the arrangements of the traditional rituals. Nandita di actually felt gratuitous of her presence in that hour of need. Anil got busy with the event manager in suggesting some minor changes, as per his refined taste. From pin to plane, he looked after all the arrangements.

Kavita went to see Saumya, while reminiscing about her as a little girl, holding a small baby doll in her tiny hands.

"Someone is looking really gorgeous," she complimented her.

In a lovely orange and magenta flared gown and with elegant make-up, Saumya looked wonderful and actually blushed when she saw her favourite *masi* there.

"Wow! Masi, you look stunning,"she exclaimed upon seeing her.

"Oh, look how time flies!It feels like it was just yesterday when you were born and I held you in my arms for the first time." Kavita still couldn't detach herself from her world of reminiscence.

"And you were just twelve then!" Nandita di said, entering the room just then and hugged Kavita. The affectionate motherly touch reminded her of being the younger one in the family again. Otherwise, in her own shell of fulfilling the many pliable roles, she had almost forgotten the child inside her. Meeting her elder sister after such a long time transported her back to that amazing time of her life.

"Di, Saumya looks so beautiful. Aayush will definitely faint tonight." Both of them smiled.

"So, how is my doll feeling?"

"Masi, I've got butterflies fluttering in my stomach and you are pulling my leg here."

There room was full of laughter and merriment .

The razzmatazz went on. Guests arrived at the venue one after the other. It was a big flamboyant Punjabi style engagement ceremony. Aayush and his family arrived soon with all the pomp and show. Both the families followed the set patterns of rituals and formalities. It being an arranged affair, Aayush and Saumya were not very open to each other. In fact, till then, they hadn't had much time to spend together. The matrimony website where they had matched, only gave the basic details about each person's personality, but it is only time that can help understand an individual really. As everything was already planned well ahead, the event moved on smoothly with the flow.

Finally, the rings were exchanged and two almost strangers got engaged to each other. Then started the practice of offering sweets to the prospective couple by everyone. The amount of sweets being stuffed inside their mouths was beyond explanation.

When all the rituals of the ceremony got over, the torturous photography session started. And then, how could the married men leave the poor bachelor boy, who was about to get married, alone? So Ayush's ragging session started soon after. He had a tough time listening to all the instructions, concerns and suggestions regarding successful marriage mantras from them. It seemed as if all the married men were enlightening him with the 'Do's and Don'ts' of married life. The poor couple could not get the least time to spend with each other. Kavita masi then came to their rescue.

"Guys! Let them enjoy little bit of their courtship period now. Have you forgotten your own? This is a life time opportunity for a couple, especially in arranged marriages."

Everyone started sharing their memories. But the raconteur this time was none other than Anil. He described his own time in such a way that all eyes were stuck on Kavita. All of a sudden, Aayush stood up and announced a couple dance to be done by Kavita and Anil. Kavita tried to refuse, but to her surprise, Anil had taken the baton in his hands. He took her hand in his and started singing.

"Soniye tere gore luc te,

Teri saree ka bejod faal,

Fikka sara jahan lagda,

Jadon nachdi tu mere naal."

(Oh beauty! The way you have tucked your saree at your fair waist.

When you dance with me, the whole world seems to be a waste.)

Kavita was completely taken by surprise. Anil, having no care for his surrounding, just wanted to dance to the rhythm. It was quite the right time to tell his wife that there was something which had gone missing between them. He knew he could touch the strings of his wife's heart with that song. He continued to sing:

"Mere bolne ki baat nahin,

Ye to nazrein hi kehti hain

Yun hi nhi guzaare soniye

Tere sang umr ke itne saal

Tu hai paas hi mere, lekin

Dur-dur lagti hai kyun.

Jo khone laga tere mere beech

Zara ab to usko sambhaal."

(It is not necessary to say something, when eyes can very well understand each other. After all, we have spent such a long period of time together. You seem to be so close, yet you have gone beyond my reach. That thing which is missing now, just don't let it go, don't let it go.)

Everybody's feet tapped to the thrill and excitement of Anil's words and tune. It was after a long time that Kavita was seeing Anil in his old style. She reckoned with the lack of togetherness in their life. Her husband had kept his viewpoint in public and his eyes were still waiting for her reply. She tried to evade her feelings, but the truth was that she herself had been searching for a solution. Amidst the gathering, she suddenly felt herself aloof. Each cell of her brain pushed to transport her back to the days when she had just finished her post graduation in Commerce. She had wanted to take up research further, but her father was in a rush to get her married. Within no time, matrimony advertisements had been sent to different newspapers. They received endless letters in response. After much scrutiny, Anil's proposal was accepted. Being too old to handle things anymore, Kavita's parents had handed over the responsibility to Nandita *di.* A formal meeting was fixed. Anil, along with his parents and elder sister, Aayesha, came to meet her then. The meeting went pretty well and both the parties accepted the match. Neither Anil, not Kavita were given much time to talk.

"Mamma, Mamma…." Tanvi's voice pulled her back to the present moment. "Aren't they looking adorable?"

The new couple was dancing romantically to a nocturne, in each other's arms on the dance floor. Kavita looked at them impressed and then turned her loving gaze to Anil. Deep in his eyes, she could see the vacuum of her life.

Chapter 5

That Sleepless Night

They returned from that wonderful evening very late that night. After changing, everyone went to their respective rooms. The next day being a Sunday, Kavita was at ease. She switched off her alarm and cleared the mess that her children had created in a hurry to enter into their beds. Dead tired after the long day, everyone soon slept. Kavita switched off the lights and entered her room. Anil had switched on the T.V. but was waiting for Kavita. "Oh! You are still awake," she asked surprised while getting into bed. Without replying, Anil looked deep into her eyes with a penetrating lust. Then he took her in his arms and kissed her. He seldom expressed his love verbally, yet his eyes often spoke impressively about his feelings. Those intimate moments with him made her feel extremely pampered. She enjoyed every bit of it, despite being dead tired. At times, such moments rejuvenate the self, depending upon the person's state of mind. Anil slept comfortably after that, but sleep turned mutinous for her that night.

She kept looking at him and kept thinking about the song he had sung at the engagement party. She knew that her husband would never speak about his feelings openly with her but he had an unbeatable capability of molding his feelings into words. And that's exactly what he had done that evening in front of so many people. She suddenly realized that off late, she had stopped listening to her husband's diary which he used to read out to her whenever she had the time. With sarcasm, she uttered the word 'time' again. She looked for his diary in his drawer and flipped through it. She read a piece of a small Punjabi song, which read:

Raati te tu sam jaani he,main tuk tuk raah takna

Savere teri pehli huvaak bachyan de kol hunddi.

Shaman teriyan saariyan maan pyo de naal hunddi

Tenu vekh vekh main iss dil vich aah bharna"

(During sleepless nights, I wait for you, but you are not there. Your mornings are for the kids and evenings for the parents. I crave for you but you are not there..)

She realized in a jiffy that there was definitely something which had gone missing between them over a period of time. Those long years of responsibilities had left them yearning for each other. She herself felt the craving to meet him once again. The sleepless night advanced with a flashback of her own life with him.

After their engagement, it was a huge thing for her to get his contact number. She had a mastermind working in all directions to crack the deal by hook or crook. One of his office friends had helped her for it. It took her almost fifteen days to finally make it. When she first made him a call, he could not believe it. He realised that his intended bride was a complete package of surprises, full of mysteries. Her chirpy and bubbly style of talking and the gesture of sending him greetings almost every week at his office really charmed him. His colleagues teased him about it, but he enjoyed it all. At times, he would not take her calls, but she never missed making them anyway. He liked everything about her, but he would never express his feelings. In his diary, however, he wrote many ghazals on her

"*Wo pehlu mein mere baithe muskura kar,*

Unhe dekhta rahun yun hi paas bitha kar

Hale dil kyun zahir karun main zubaan se

Ai dil tu hi bataa de unke paas jaakar."

(I would love to see her sitting and smiling forever, 'cause I love her so much. When my heart is with her, what need is there to speak out my feelings. My heart can tell her everything.)

Her ebullience always escalated his feelings for her. The more they talked, the more their bonding improved. She reminisced about her courtship period when they had hardly met each other thrice, but each of those meetings were carved inside her heart. She had found Anil a very balanced person. That period is undoubtedly a cakewalk for newly engaged couples.

Arrange marriages are like mystery novels. With each turning page, the story passes through unbelievable twists and turns. After they got married, their life was far away from a'happily ever after'. Life is not a fairy tale. It is a mix of all hues, a blend of all colours. Happiness is the way of life and sorrow, the spice of life. Enjoying all the good things together, while also accepting all odd things about each other, is not an easy job. All this is part and parcel of any relationship in the world. Be it love marriage or arranged, the two different individuals always need to work together to hone their relationship. Kavita and Anil shared a good adjustment time together. Their honeymoon period, however, had lasted only for a few days as Tanay was conceived during their honeymoon itself. Although, both of them were not prepared to start a family yet, they had to continue with this new phase of their life, parenthood, due to external pressures. Kavita actually enjoyed her would-be-mother phase of life. Both of them managed to find time for each other, walked around hand in hand and ate those spicy *golgappas* together. She felt herself very lucky to be blessed with such a lovely family. Aayesha *di* was one of the most sensible sisters-in-law she found in her new family. She had been married and settled in New York. Despite being just two years elder to Anil, she was a motherly figure to him. Anil could still enter into an argument with his mother for once, but with Aayesha *di*, he could never even think of it. Kavita rectified the negative image of 'in-laws' that she had bore all the while in her mind, after her marriage. Usually, we form a perspective as per our surroundings and the general notion that prevails is that 'in-laws' can never be parents, but Kavita's in-laws proved it wrong. Soon after, Tanay, their little bundle of joy, entered their life and the partners of life turned into parents for life. Dirty nappies and baby odour became a regular part of their lives. Their share of responsibilities kept piling up from then on. Her grown protruding belly and odious feelings about herself made her quite reclusive. The very next year, Tanvi was born too. Anil got industriously busy with his job. In a nutshell, both of them found themselves indulged in their separate responsibilities.

How do we perceive life in terms of phases? Infancy, childhood, adolescence, adulthood, middle age, old age, etc?But life is more than just these phases. It is about living each phase to the fullest ,and parenthood is that part of a married life which is wholly a learning period. Parents, being two separate individuals, might hold very different opinions about parenting. Getting a common consensus about parenting then needs a lot of patience and adjustment between the couple. Sometimes ingenious, sometimes ingenuous; life is doubtlessly strange.

It was not that Kavita and Anil were imprudent towards each other, rather, they tried to improvise as per the conditions of their life. Kavita joined a teaching job as soon as the kids started going to school. Time then started to run faster than ever before. Their kids' schooling, their homework, the advancing age of her in-laws and their retirements, everything happened so quickly, as if the events had been prescheduled elsewhere, unnoticed by them.

Strange! The precursor stays off the stage and the characters keep performing the prescient events with a guarded guidance of no one but themselves. Apparently, we enjoy all the events, whether good or bad, and accept all changes in our lives with great comfort and ease.

Both of them kept lubricating their lives with love and care and accepted life with all its hues, whether grey or green. Life was loveable, for they were together.

Together. She smiled to herself as she evaluated her life in the light of their togetherness. However, she found herself betrayed by her own life as all her younger years had flown by, while she had not been able to live her life to the fullest with the person she loved the most. *Was that good enough to relish?* "No," she muttered. It was time to redefine her love, she decided. She was all set to purloin time from her life. With exuberance in her eyes, she shut her eyelids, in hope to pursue the makeover waiting for her ahead.

Chapter 6

The Unusual Meeting

"Hi, Kavita." Kavita turned back to see who had called her.

"OMG, Aparna?Unbelievable. Is that really you?" Kavita stood up in surprise.

The ecstasy between them was evident as they hugged each other. For some moments, Kavita felt like she was living her own life again. After all, the two friends had met each other after sixteen years. Strange! Girls adapt to the new environment after marriage in such a manner that their old relationships are left nurtured. Yet, even after that long a gap, their bond had remained unaffected. Aparna was her best friend and had been in the same town for two years, and Kavita had no idea about it. Kavita called up her mom-in-law and freed herself for the next two hours. Then, both of them went to a coffee shop nearby.

"So Aparna, what's up? Where have you been? What about your husband, children and what are you doing these days? Tell me everything!"

"Oh *jaaneman*! You have not changed at all. Let me breathe properly first. Such a long array of queries you have. We've met after ages. Let's order two cappuccinos, and then we can talk."

"Fine!" Kavita ordered two cappuccinos with brownies, which used to be their favourite hangout meal once upon a time.

While sipping coffee, Aparna opened her heart to Kavita. "I broke up with Somesh. His torturous travelling job was not easy for me to handle. It started getting on my nerves. My son, Aarnav, studies at a boarding school now and I am enjoying my regained single status. I took a job at a multinational bank. It is better to grab the opportunities when they knock at your door. Otherwise, life becomes too dull. I felt myself so lost in those responsibilities and expectations, and then this job happened." Aparna continued to justify her life and decisions in her own way.

Kavita remained calm and patient while listening to everything. *Listening*, she had learnt over a period of time, was better than speaking. At that point of time, she had no words to express her opinion towards relationships. It was rather difficult for her to accept this new avatar of her best friend. It was unbelievable for her to see how arrogant a person could become when love was out of their life. She couldn't come to terms with the fact that it was the same friend who was famous for her cool attitude in college and who's relationship with Somesh was vouched for by everyone. The love guru of her college days was now talking ill about relationships. Confounded, she watched Aparna taking a fag, sipping her coffee and talking senselessly about the burdens of a relationship.

Those two hours which she had thought would rejuvenate her, became the worst two hours of her life. She came to realize the importance of the unconditional grace which surrounded her life. She could feel the pace at which her love had been growing with each passing day. Her mundane routine, the catfights between the siblings and the generation gap in her house which often got on her nerves, suddenly started to look baseless at that time. In fact, those things were important to keep her attached to this life. She could see how living for one's own self could make a person as arid as a desert. She could connect the barren eyes of her friend with the dryness of the life that she was living. More than anything, she felt sorry in her heart for her friend's approach towards life. Maybe, Aparna was unwilling to accept that life, in its true sense, is to love and not to crib. Kavita was never in favour of meekly accepting any kind of boundaries over oneself, but she strongly believed that love should be unconditional, and that wherever love flows, there remains no space for arrogance. Yet, each individual has one's own parameters to live within. Without interfering in Aparna's life, she chose to be a quite listener. Though, this 'calm listening' helped her empower her own mind and enabled her to see life with a different perspective. On reaching home, she found herself thinking about her husband's piece of mind which he had recorded in his diary.

"Love has to surely glow between us," she thought. "This vacuum has no place in our lives and I'll not fall prey to the cruelty of 'time' anymore." Her eyes sparkled with a stupid idea that suddenly flashed in her mind. With a calm smile, she resumed the usual way of her life.

Anil had to go to Rakshanda's house to get some documents signed by her. Being unwell, she had opted to stay at home that day. The documents were confidential and needed to reach her safely, so Anil decided that while going back home, he would personally do the needful. While driving to her house, he turned on the radio. Interspersedly, he would laugh at the fun filled comments of livelyRJ's. Undoubtedly, laughter is the best therapy to cope with the everyday pressure. He stopped his car right outside Rakshanda's penthouse. He looked in the mirror before getting down. The grey in his hair irked him a bit, but at that time he had no alternative. He rang the doorbell and a maid servant opened the door. She led him in and asked him to wait in the drawing room. He sat there quietly, and marvelled at the expensive décor. The place looked nice but not entirely warm or welcoming. The vibrations of the place told a different story about the owner of the house. He had always admired the lady for her warm gestures and an aesthetically pleasant appearance. But while waiting for her, he started to form a completely different opinion of her. She came in insipidly dressed and was unwilling to show even the most basic courtesy to the guest. Deliberately avoiding the regular pleasantries, she asked him for the required documents. After signing them, she handed them over coldly to Anil and her gestures clearly signaled that she wanted him to leave. Anil left for his house, surprised and taken back by Rakshanda's cold attitude.

"She could at least have offered some water. What a strange person!" he thought. His views about the lady had changed in an instant. This unusual meeting forced him to compare her with his wife. He found himself admire Kavita's habit of making others comfortable in her company. It was definitely her strength. She had always been so dutiful, that she never thought about herself before others. Her selfless attitude was what made her so beautiful. Anil realised her love around him.

What a coincidence? Both Kavita and Anil had gone through some bitter experiences to realise the better part of their better halves. Kavita could not resist admiring her husband's passionate love for her and Anil could not stop appreciating his wife's unconditional support for him and his family. This realization was so fulfilling for both of them. A marriage is actually the most satisfying experience for those who appreciate the quality time they get to spend with their partners. No matter if time betrays, responsibilities become immaterial when life partners admire and appreciate each other's unasked and unsaid support. Both of them underwent the same feelings of gratefulness towards each other. Love was in the air. This gratitude merged with a feeling of being together and celebrating their love. Both found themselves on a guilt trip together to weigh their relationship again. Unknowingly, Aparna and Rakshanda had ignited the dormant feelings of love in them. The urge of being together was finding its place in their heart again. In their heart of hearts, however, they thanked their stars for those unusual meetings.

Chapter 7

The Lost Love Affair

Anil drove home, bearing in him those mixed feelings of guilt and gratefulness. He entered the house that evening with the same kind of expression which he used to carry during the initial days of their marriage. His eyes were looking forward to spend some beautiful moments with her, while her eyes looked at him with the same feelings too. Things went on as usual, but their perception was unusual this time. After a long time they found themselves fascinated by this new experience. Each of their bitter encounters had opened up their insight about relationships and they were earnest to involve each other in this new found inner freedom. The evening chores were taken care of as per routine and everyone came to sit at the dining table for dinner as usual. She had prepared the family favourite chicken *biryani*, and they all enjoy it dearly. As Anil put the chicken leg piece in his mouth, Kavita could not help but giggle. It was not her usual way of behaving, so she tried to contain her feelings. It was a little awkward in front of the elders, as well as the youngsters. On entering their room after wrapping up the dinner, she recited a Punjabi couplet with the most passionate expressions that she could muster.

"Tuaade layi sartaaj mere, main zindagi guzaar chaddi,

Tuanu saare change lagde, khande chicken de naal haddi,

Main kede kede paase jaavan, jawab tusi deo menu,

Ki gal vich paaya jeda dhol, oohne ta hai vajna."

(Dear, I have lived my life for you, but you only want to live with everyone else. You like chicken with bone and want me to be with you alone. But when we are knee-deep in responsibilities, how do I leave everything for you? Everyone has to bear their share of responsibilities, specially if we have chosen them ourselves.)

Anil looked at her and smiled at her witty creativity. With eyes full of mischief, they entered their room.

"So, you read my diary?"

"Hmmm! After a long time."

Anil wanted to measure the depth of her love in her eyes.

"Do you still love me with the same passion?" he asked.

"I need nothing else when you are around. I live you in each moment of my life," Kavita could feel each pore of her body singing out for him.

Those shared passionate and blissful moments shed away their long-held grudges towards each other, and the unconditional love that they originally had for each other, resurfaced again. With no pseudo feelings, pure love flowed between them again. They talked to each other about their day's events, the strange meetings and their monotonous routines. They even reminisced about their lost love and their feelings which had lost all their lustre. Sometimes, things that seem most difficult are actually so easy to handle. All you need is a good talk!

Time was ticking away, yet they sat reliving their everlasting memories in dim lights and with low music on. Kavita pulled out some old photo albums. It was really amazing for both of them to peep into their life after so long through the little window of that album. Till the time it hadn't been opened, the memories lay silently beneath the surface, but as they open it, all the brackets let loose, refreshing them once again. They fondly cherished their old times and Kavita got hooked to a photograph all of a sudden. It was from when they had been on their first surprise date after their engagement. It transported them to 16 years ago.

Kavita had just finished her post graduation and was waiting for the results to come out, along with her friends at college. At that time, connectivity through mobile or internet was only a dream. All of a sudden, Anil showed up and said, "Hi." Her friends tried to pull her out of her imaginative world, but she was flying high with the promise of a new life. 'A new dove in love', her friends had named her. After the results were announced, they both went out for coffee. It was the first time they were meeting privately, and the rendezvous got inscribed in her heart forever. It was after this meeting that the arranged courtship started to transform into a love relationship. Blinded by love, they found it hard to recall their lives from before they had met each other.

"Let's start it all over again," Kavita said, finding that moment quite appropriate to reveal her stupid but sweet idea to her husband and to convince him of its importance.

"What?" Anil asked.

"The lost love affair."

"Are you kidding?"

"No, we are missing out on this us-time and we won't be able to get it unless we snatch it out of our busy schedules."

"What about our children and parents?"

"Let's not disclose our affair to them."

"So, are you going to hide this from Mama?"

"Not just me, you'll need to hide it from everyone too."

There was a brief word-less pause between them.

Kavita's eyes had lit-up with the same old mischief that Anil had recently been longing for.

"But madam, I'm turning 40 and you are no longer in your youth either," he said, still reluctant to follow through with her weird idea.

"Age is just a figure. It cannot be a deciding factor for anything. Let us just live our own life. Imagine life 20 years from now, when our kids will be settled in their own worlds and we would not longer be able to pull off the things we can still do now. Look at these Bollywood actors and actresses, is age ever a factor for them? No. Then why should we allow age to come between us? Think about it, how can we let time victimize our relationship?"

She had her own style of convincing him.

Her college-time spunk was back. Her expressions and her mind, more like a passionate lover at that moment, prioritised only their togetherness and nothing beyond it. This, adding onto her chirpy and witty words, made the whole atmosphere very lively. "Let us design our own destiny from here on. If not now, then when will we do it? Oh, my messenger of love! You are the one who were, are and will always reign over my heart. Everyone will move on with their lives, but we will stay, simply craving to enjoy together. I wish that when we grow old, we are able to fondle our sweet memories and not repent taking each other for granted, due to the burden of responsibilities on us. To be with you, is all I want. To live with you, is all I wish," she concluded, looking hopefully at her husband to approve of her plan.

Anil found himself rolling on the floor after listening to his wife's theatrical speech on love, and in such a melodramatic style too. Her expressions had tickled that missing streak inside him. He was seeing her chirping that same old way after a very long time. Still, he did not look all that convinced with her idea. The reason behind his reluctance was their age, and that they would have to play hide and seek, just to meet and spend time with each other. Although, he knew that his near and dear ones were actually oblivious to the vacuum that had generated between Kavita and himself. It was, in f act, impossible to make them realize that they had, unknowingly, been the ones to cleave them apart in the first place. Kavita read in his eyes this hitch towards starting a secretive affair together. Yet, she was not ready to give up in trying to convince him further.

"Dear, we have only one life and we have only lived it for others till now. I am not willing to continue surrendering it to the needs of others anymore. All I ask for is just some stolen moments for ourselves. It will be difficult to explain this to the people related to us, so it will be better if we don't disclose it to them at all. Sounds adventurous, doesn't it? Think over it, what if you start feeling good in someone else's company, or if I find someone else to share my problems with, what will we do then? But why should we even get involved in such an ordeal? Come on! Let us start an affair of our own. We would meet each other like lovers. You'd wait for me at a coffee shop with orchids and I'd dress up all fancy to impress you. Please, say yes. Please! Please! It will be so thrilling," she said, glancing at him passionately.

A brief silence resumed again.

Kavita held his hands in hers, removed his spectacles and rested her face on his chest, while looking deep into his eyes. "I miss you," she said. Anil knew exactly what she meant. He wrapped his arms around her and whispered back gently, "Me too." Life had given them a fair chance to live together, yet the irony of time was that they missed each other, despite having lived under the same roof for years. Anil was somehow convinced about her proposal. He shut his eyes for a few moments. Kavita understood that her husband was about to speak his mind and was just taking some time to assimilate the situation. She waited patiently, while Anil's fingers gently stroked her hair. She could feel his heartbeats on her face. Somewhere deep in his heart, a child had opened his glittering eyes and said, "Let's do it." Anil finally agreed to the proposal and said, "Yes!" With a sigh of achievement, Kavita closed her eyes to fall into a peaceful sleep.

Chapter 8

The Special Date

To become aware of a problem is problematic. Sorting life after realizing its need, however, is not all that difficult. Kavita and Anil arrived at a consensus on making certain changes in their routine engagements to adjust their meetings without hampering anyone's schedule. They planned to meet every Friday evening. They made a few necessary arrangements, like opening new accounts with the names Kavi and Neel, hiring a tuition teacher for the children, and finding a maid to make chapattis, etc. Using WhatsApp to talk to each other was fairly dicey as the kids were grown up and often used her mobile for their own purposes. However, chatting online was fun. It re-invented the romance between them and this time, it was tech-savvy too.

"Hi Kavi, are you there?"

"Hi Neel, what's up?"

"Nothing much, at office."

"I hope you remember our special date tomorrow."

"Yeah! First one like this."

"What have you planned?"

Why should I disclose it?

"Okay. Would you be able to manage it?

"Uh! Let's see."

The next day was the first Friday since they had agreed to start their secret affair. Alas! It had all been too easy to think, but far more difficult to actually manage. Hiding a romance is never a cake walk, no matter what the age. To avoid any kind of a last minute hassle, she fabricated a story for her mom-in-law.

"Mamma, remember I told you about my friend Aparna? She has invited me to her place tomorrow evening. I'll go thereafter Tanay returns from his tuitions. I've told Claccy to make chapattis for dinner."

Krishna ji had never interfered unnecessarily in their life. It was just that she was unaware of the fact that her son and daughter-in-law had started to feel victimized due to the lack of time they had for each other. Despite not being a stereotypical mom-in-law, she was oblivious towards her responsibility of understanding that time constraint between them. She had never let any kind of her own insecurities hamper her children's progress. In fact, when Kavita took the responsibilities of the house on her own shoulders, she had been thrilled to hand it over to her. However, she did not realize when the gap between the generations grew to such an extent that it became a major disturbance in the house. Moreover, at her age, she never thought of giving any justification at all for her behaviour. After all, she expected her experience to command respect from everyone in the house. As there was no awareness about any kind of an unrest between Kavita and Anil in the house, there was no room for any realization regarding the need to work upon that problem either. She could never think or believe, even in her wildest imaginations, that Kavita was lying to her. As always, she was quite a sport.

Kavita was thrilled about her first secretive date. She went to her room, noticed the grey streak in her hair and thought of tinting it dark again. Then, she glanced at her wardrobe and searched for something nice to wear. Finally, she decided to don a smart black top with her long denim skirt. She also took out a new stole, which she had originally bought for Tanvi. Just like a newly hooked spinster, she rehearsed her look in front of the mirror.

"Wow! Not bad...where have you been hiding, dear?"

She appreciated herself, the lost version of her life. She felt so wonderful to finally bring out her scared, hidden self and reshape her own personality again. She enjoyed being herself. That brand new experience of meeting her own SELF boosted her self esteem. Isn't that strange? We spend so much of our time thinking about others, but when it comes to our own Self, it is the least favoured person. Our attitude towards the Self remains that of negligence. It is perhaps the fear of being labeled as selfish, or maybe we are conditioned to not take care of the Self. She actually realized at that time that with a little attention and care to one's Self, a sense of belongingness with the Self can be developed easily. The Self gains maturity only after confronting its inhibitions. It was the sense of that maturity that gave her a new height. The alarm on her mobile rang. It was time for the children to come back. She packed up her stuff and put it away before anyone could realize this makeover. She rearranged herself back into her role of a mother, but without hiding her Self this time.

She asked Tanay about his day and checked Tanvi's home assignments. While dealing with all the household chores that day, she found herself quite relaxed, more than she had ever felt before. After all, she had enjoyed some super moments with herself after a long period of time.

"Mamma," Tanvi interrupted her fancies, "Why are there so many stories about girls being so submissive, and give all authority to the so called 'Prince Charmings'. Are they such dumbos that they can't even guard themselves?"

"Sweetheart, it is always up to you to change such stereotypes and make the Prince Charming deserve the princess. Let us make the princess so strong that she can decide her own fate. Actually, for ages we have been told to accept such things and we blindly agreed to it, but these days, girls like you have started questioning the age old traditions about such gender roles. It's a really good practice too."

Tanay smiled and said, "But Mamma, girls are still not so strong, physically and emotionally. They cry easily."

"Son," she smiled and replied, "Girls should only shed tears for those who deserve it. Moreover, if boys feel emotional and want to cry, they can do it too. It is time we leave these gender issues behind and think about the capabilities of people as human beings. We should evolve as human beings, be stronger emotionally, mentally and physically, irrespective of whatever gender we are. If a human being is determined, he/she can drink the ocean or can change the face of the mountains, no matter what gender they are. So both of you should be focused and determined. Strive to be human with the strength of your character."

Their mother's powerful words made a deep impression on their tender hearts and made the teenagers feel really stronger. Kavita felt that their thought process was still at an evolving stage and needed positive reinforcement in the right direction. As a mother, she felt she was doing her job to the maximum extent of her ability. At least she was not vegetating her time away, although sometimes, this tough task of being a home-maker frustrated her in terms of the drift it caused between her wishes and duties.

The next day was the day of the 'planned Date'. It being a second Saturday the next day, the workload on the kids was lesser than usual. She planned the entire day's chores in such a manner that her evening was completely free. She also instructed Claccy auntie to make the chapattis. As scheduled, she got ready in her rehearsed dress with tremendous zeal glittering in her eyes. Everyone was really surprised to witness this makeover. It was not their fault at all. Kavita had always abstained from self indulgence due to her full time job as a home-maker. In that capacity, it was difficult for her to make her near and dear ones comprehend her thoughts and feelings. But now, she had bid adieu to her old mundane routine and opened her arms wide to embrace an exiting time ahead.

With an exquisite grace about her, she entered 'Cookie's Coffee Point' before time. To her surprise, she found Anil entering from the other gate just then, looking at her with eyes full of affection. That admiring look expressed his adulation for her, which she accepted gracefully. With all due courtesies in place, he pulled a chair for her and asked her to take a seat. She felt quite fascinated by the ambience around her.

"Cappuccino with brownies?" he winked to catch her expression. She batted her eyelashes at him, as if asking him, "Oh! You remember?"

Time is dynamic, but those moments were static. They kept looking at each other, reliving their fond memories from the past. Love thrives beyond circumstances, boundaries, relationships and individuals. They maintained their promise of not discussing their routines, so that there was enough space to talk about other things, like their hobbies, interests and of course, music. Anil loved to express his feelings in words, but was equally interested in instrumental music. He loved to play the guitar. Kavita realized it and asked him to pick up a guitar on display at the eatery, being used there as a marketable feature. The love birds were truly enjoying their freedom and spontaneity. He started singing:

"Pal do pal mein jo hota hai,

Wo pyar nahin wo nasha hai.

Jo waqt ke saath nikharta hai,

Uss pyar mein hi to mazaa hai."

(That which happens in moments, is not love, but only infatuation. The love that matures slowly with Time is the actual fascination.)

Main basa lun tujhe nigahon mein aise,

Ki tasveeron ki bhi zaroorat na ho.

Meri har aarzoo mein ho khushbu teri,

Bas yun hi mujhe teri aadat na ho.

Ye zindagi tere saath hai to khuda hai,

Jo tu na ho paas to jeena hi sazaa hai."

(I don't need pictures to remember you by, for you reside in my eyes. Your fragrance is not just a habit, it is my fascination. Living with you is no less than Godly bliss, and to be away form you is punishment.)

It was truly a wonderful evening. They talked about everything, but relationships. While talking to each other, Anil suddenly noticed the beautiful 'choker' around her neck.

"Wow! This is so beautiful."

"You like it? I designed it specially for this 'Date.'"

He affectionately looked into her eyes, which twinkled with love beyond their relationship. The blushing evening had infused her face with its grace.

Anil felt the need to revive Kavita's passion of jewellery designing. Strange but true! Husband and wife often become each other's needs, more than their interests. Though they had been sharing a lifetime, they never got enough time to actually know each other. This had come as a life-time opportunity for them to relive their interests, and both of them were eager to make the most of it. Their first 'date', however, made one thing dot clear in their minds, that *to reveal this secret affair to anyone was not a good idea.* On this realization, Anil held her hand and said, "Good, we shall opt for it." They soon parted ways to return to their respective routines, as neither of them could afford to get late. Going back to their routines after such a beautiful change was difficult, but they had to do it. Isn't it better to take precautions beforehand to be safe? With a promise to meet secretly once every week, they kindled those adorable moments forever in their hearts.

Chapter 9

Another Twist

The morning arrived fresh as never before. Just as leaves covered in morning dew look fresh, the droplets of that affectionate evening enlivened their attitude. All of a sudden, everything started to look appealing. The malaise in their eyes was replaced by the glittering feeling of love. Finally, they were gathering the guts to steal time for themselves. A new love saga was on the cards. No boundaries, no conditions; this is how this middle age'd love could best be defined. When there is nothing left to show and nothing to hide, when the best and the worst are all known to each other, when there is a uniqueness in being two but one, when the two are bare in front of each other, when they know the other inside out, middle age can really understand love much better than any other. At teenage, it is usually mere attraction which seeks attention, while at old age, it is mostly about companionship, but at middle age, it is filled with romance, humour, as well as the longing to touch and feel, while being at the other's side. This oneness is beautiful.

When life drives ahead full throttle during the middle age and we find ourselves engaged in financial and social responsibilities, the dip in our emotive quotient touches its lowest points and then arises the need to give it a boost. That is the time when we generally get caught in melancholy lifestyles. The same routines, same responsibilities and same factors adversely affect the mindset. An unresponsiveness to the so called CHANGE encroaches upon the immunity of relationships. The urge for this CHANGE, however, should be mutual and unadulterated.

Both of them welcomed this freshness in their lives. Meeting secretively once every week made their routines melodious. The events that used to screw up their days before, became a usual part and parcel of their lives. Eventually, love draped itself around them in all imaginative forms, which had not been possible in reality before. It was the golden chance for them to relish all their fascinations in real. Kavita tried to change her look for every meeting. After all, loving the original love was far better than being sleazy at any point of time.

There had definitely arrived a CHANGE in their lives, yet it was not so noticeable for any of the family members. Krishna ji found it a little strange that Kavita had suddenly started going out every week with her friend, but still there was no sign of doubt in her mind. Assimilating with the change in their own way, they appreciated the reduced stress in the house, with less murky mornings and lesser fussy evenings. Their routines had not changed, but due to a change in their perspectives, they looked forward to meet each other.

That day, Anil drove down to office while listening to meaningless numbers on the radio, duly curated by his favourite witty RJs. He laughed generously at each of their jokes. Even the maddening traffic rush could not put him off. With a jovial mood, he entered the office area.

"Sir, good morning! Rakshanda Madam was enquiring about you."

"Oh! Hi Nancy. How are you, dear?"

Nancy was the receptionist and she replied blushing, "Fine, Sir. You look fresh today."

Anil smiled and headed towards his office. After keeping his laptop in his cabin, he went to Rakshanda's cabin. She had contributed a great deal to his latest realization and his last experience of meeting Rakshanda at her place had changed his perception of her to a great extent. Regardless, he didn't want to be judgmental on the grounds of his perception. At times, the background and the forefront portray different realities. Thus, without harbouring any hard feelings in his heart, he knocked at her door.

"Who's that? Please come in."

"Hi, it's me. Anil."

"Oh! Hello, Anil. How are you doing? I am so sorry, I was not in a condition to attend to you when you had come to my place that evening. I really apologize."

"That's fine. I hope you have recovered now."

"Yeah! Right, but there is a problem. I need your help."

"Sure, what is it?"

"There is a conference aligned in Pune this weekend. But due to my health reasons, I don't think I will be able to make it. May I recommend your name? The management wants someone really responsible to attend it."

"Pune conference? Okay, Rakshanda. Let me check with my appointments this weekend."

"Please let me know by noon."

"Right."

Anil went back to his cabin. A mischievous plan was hatching in his brain. He checked out all his commitments and finalized this program.

He then opened his online chat window.

"Hi, Kavi. Can you come to Pune with me this weekend?"

"NO. Neel, how will that be possible? What am I going to say at home?"

"Don't worry. I'll tell you."

Kavita gasped and thought, "Anil is getting way too serious about this. Keeping a whole trip secret will be too difficult. Oh God! Sometimes these husbands just don't realize the family issues." Kavita's thought train was on a spree, but she also wished for this trip to actually be possible. She was willing to hear out Anil's plan and then again, her sensitive chords started chiming.

There is nothing wrong in doing what you want, yet why is it so difficult to make your loved ones understand your intentions? Why do people connect everything to ethics? Being lively does not necessarily mean that one is selfish. Moreover, who defines ethics for you? Is it so that following traditions is ethical, regardless of whether being traditional is logical or not? These are such long debatable issues. However, she was excited about spending two days away from this traditional psyche and strangulations. She was willing to host the unnoticed SELF above all traditions and logic. She wished to be with-in her own self-contained periphery, which repelled the world around. *At times, being selfish is not that bad*, she thought.

She desperately waited for Anil to come home.

As they entered into their room that night, she inquisitively raised her brows at him.

Seeing her questioning expression, he revealed his cards to her. "Tell them you are planning to go to Mumbai to help Nandita Di. I will say that my conference is in Ahmadabad. We will plan our tickets accordingly. Just tell Di that we are out on a family vacation, so she will not make any calls at home. As it is, all of us have our mobile phones with us, so there is no need to worry."

That was a bag full of surprises for her. Her never-so-bold husband was now designing this mutinous idea for their escape. She gulped down her hesitation with resistance. "WH…HAT?"she exclaimed completely stunned and then whispered, "Are you alright?"

"I have been thinking about this plan since noon and you are giving me such expressions now. Are you going to give up so soon? I told you it is easier said than done. Talking about an issue is very simple, but now is time to implement what we started. We'll lose our zeal again, simply discussing that we will do this, or we will do that. Just talking about sparing time for each other will not result to anything, it's all about doing, Madam. Starting a love affair at this age is as daring as taking candies away from a toddler, and now you want to take a backseat? Either give in, or give up."

She kept looking at her husband, perplexed at how he was talking the same way as she had done to convince him to start their affair in the first place.

Ah! She did not know how to react. She had no other option but to give in.

"Ibtadaye puraana ishq hai, rota hai kya

Aage aage dekhite jaaiye hota hai kya."

(It is just the start of the old love, for which you make such hue and cry. Just wait and watch how life unfolds further.)

Not very sure about her thoughts still, she agreed to be a part of the plan, wondering what kind of twists and turns her life was taking. Besides everything else, however, the very thought of spending a few days with her love, tickled at her nerves.

Chapter 10

The Subtle Change

On another usual morning, Anil set the stage for a super melodrama at home. After all, he was brushing up on his college time acting skills. Kavita was part of the scene too, but she was actually scared of getting caught. Sipping his cup of tea at the dining table, he asked Kavita, "Don't you think you should go to Mumbai to help Nandita Di with Saumya's wedding shopping? She has been calling you over and over again."

She looked at Krishna ji to read her face and then tried her own artistic streak, saying, "How can I go, Anil? I have to look after the house and can't leave everything just like that. I know Di will not mind it, as she is well aware of my commitments here," she blurted out in a single breath.

"That is why she called me and asked me for permission to release you for some time. Now you tell me, am I holding you here? Do you really need my permission to go anywhere? Have I ever stopped you from doing anything?" His pitch was higher than usual, as if there was some resentment in him for something he had not liked.

It was commendable, she thought. Never had she imagined even in her wildest fancies that her husband was such a fine actor and that he would play the love game so seriously. She lauded him in her heart while he continued to speak.

"Listen, I am going to leave for a conference in Ahmadabad. If you wish, you can also plan for Mumbai this weekend. I'll leave early morning on Saturday. You can also plan accordingly." He looked at her expectantly as it was her turn to speak her dialogue, but she was lost somewhere in her own thoughts.

"Perfect planning," she said, her mind still clouded by disbelief, as if whatever she had just heard was only a dream.

"Kavita...Kavita, where are you lost?" Krishna ji nudged her back to the present.

"Oh! So sorry, Mamma! I was just thinking about something,"she said, pretending to be unsure of the program.

"If you want to go, then you should make your plan. I'll take care of the house, while the kids are grown up enough to take care of themselves in most ways. Their tuition teacher can see to their studies and I'll tell Claccy to make food. It is just a matter of two days. Don't worry, we will manage. Just instruct Tanay to listen to me before leaving," Krishna ji offered her help, like any other concerned mother would.

Now that was a clean bold! Kavita's eyes missed to blink as she looked at her husband and then at her mother-in-law. Without any court proceedings, the case had turned in her favour. She was no longer required to be a part of that examination. With a sanction of this unexpected leave in hand, she was on cloud nine with exaltation.

The melodrama had gotten over with a winning smile on their faces and more than anything else, not a single trace of doubt was left anywhere.

Carried away by emotions, she went into her room and pinched herself. She couldn't believe that she was actually going for an excursion with her love. She decided that it was time to refresh her wardrobe and spend liberally on each moment of the trip. She recalled the words of her mother-in-law. "It is just a matter of two days," she had said. **TWO** full days. A smile danced across her face. She took out all her savings, the money she had saved for a rainy day. Sometimes, in pursuit to fulfil our responsibilities, we set our priorities in such a way that we end up sacrificing our wishes. She felt the need to change her perception towards her priorities. It is no doubt difficult to challenge your own idiosyncrasies, but one can always try to be flexible. She took quite a time in thinking and accepting the change. With a satisfactory smile, she mellowed down to the mystical power of love.

Saturday was approaching and she found herself feeling a little apprehensive about leaving everything for her own selfish interest. But was she really being selfish, she thought. The dilemma disturbed her, but she tried hard to justify her stand. Even though everyone in the house was supportive, she felt it a little too difficult to let go.

A new message flashed on her FB chat. "They are happy in their own lives. Give them their space, Kavi. You deserve to be happy too. Move on, dear." Anil had sensed her vibes and sent this message to elevate her mood.

"Oh! Thank you so much." A tear rolled down her cheek. It was difficult to play so many roles and justice to them in one single life.

Anil booked separate taxies for the two of them such that everyone at home would believe that they were going to separate destinations. For her, however, it was altogether a dreamy sequence. The airbus was jam-packed, but this honeymoon couple was deeply engrossed in just one other. It was after a gap of 15 years that they were finally alone together, free from all kinds of responsibilities and bondages. Both of them relived the memories of their first honeymoon. *Shimla*, their first honeymoon destination, was a most popular spot at that time. Things had changed a lot over the years and so did the vacation plans. It was not that they never went on vacations after marriage, but with a bag full of responsibilities pulling them down, it never turned out to be their kind a of holiday. Reminiscent of their first trip together, they shared a generous laugh. Kavita had been like a doll of wax and Anil had found himself treading on egg shells with regard to her. She was a chirpy, lively and self confident girl, yet wearing those raunchy post-wedding outfits in front of Anil would always spread a blush on her face, which further used to make Anil feel guilty of touching her. The best thing was that while walking hand in hand at mall road, they would often see couples locking lips with each other, but never dared to do it themselves. Going by the ideal definition of true love, as that of a soul meeting another soul, they did not let themselves feel free enough to display it in public. To even discuss the parameters defining love as provocatively displayed at the Ajanta and Ellora caves was a taboo at that time, while Kamasutra, as depicted by Vatsayana, was a tricky issue to talk on. So, newly married and not so open with each other, the couple could only laugh nervously as such things.

But things were very different this time. There was a unique kind of chemistry between them, a strength of bonding that had developed over the years, when one's own emotions are attached to the partner's state of mind. The expression and repeated assurance of it is not that important at that stage. The physical and emotional compatibility matures with each moment spent together. Ego clashes slowly disappear because winning or losing an argument becomes unimportant, as a relationship of oneness is beyond any measure. For Kavita and Anil, there was definitely something different in the air. They felt themselves returning to their youth. It was a most wonderful flight for them. From the airport, they hired a cab. Sitting in the back seat of the cab, they folded their arms into each other's and she rested her head on his shoulder. They enjoyed this newfound freedom, looking into each other's eyes.

Anil had to attend the conference, but he was not so keen on leaving Kavita alone at the hotel room. He tried to hide his emotions, but Kavita read his mind. To save him from his embarrassment, she planned her time herself and discussed it with him. Then, she held his hand in hers and asked, "Anil, why are you so worried about leaving me alone here?"

"Hey! How did you read my mind?"

"Dear, you don't need to think twice before telling me anything. We both have this understanding."Anil admired his wife's intent and looked at her with affection.

Love is realized best when you give it, more than you demand from it. That's the basic prerequisite to love and to be loved. A relationship can best be relished when there is no burden in giving because if it is burdensome, you are not truly in love. Anil and Kavita felt b

Chapter 11

The Matured Love

After taking some rest, she booked an appointment at the hotel's spa. Her savings that she had got with her were to be optimally used. It was time to rejuvenate and recollect those golden years, while living in the beautiful present. With some lovely self-indulgence and pampering, she felt the final result was quite stupendous. The glowing face, shiny hair and some beautifully done nail art greatly enhanced her beauty. For the evening, she changed into a blush maroon evening gown and paired it with a silk choker around her neck. The charming dusk lit up a twilight on her face, making her look all the more seductive. She lit some candles in their room and dropped a few drops of geranium oil on the wicks of the candles. She was ready to seduce him that night, in the perfect ambience.

On the other side, Anil was growing more and more desperate to reach the hotel room after his conference. As soon as he entered inside, he broke into a frenzy. She told him to control, and whispered *Kiss* in his ears. *Keep it slow and steady*. He picked her up in his arms and took her to bed while gently caressing her. She melted in his arms and he touched her at all the right places to reach her heart and soul. After the frisky moments, they found themselves looking into each others' eyes and expressed their deep rooted love. They talked endlessly about pleasure, be it physical, material or spiritual. "Spiritual?" Anil asked Kavita, "What do you mean by spiritual pleasure?" "Dear husband," she smiled, "Seeking pleasure and avoiding pain is our basic nature. When we chose our work field, either as a professional, or a housewife, or a labourer, it is the work that guides us to move ahead with conviction. The work done by us explains our character. Being self contained and satisfied, while surrendering to the results, is being spiritual. It is not easy for the women folk to fulfil all their responsibilities without the help of that unforeseen support. That support is the pillar on which this society stands."

"And how can you interrelate sex with spirituality?" he asked, surprised.

"Why do we consider sex a bad thing? It is a form of human hunger or thirst. All our senses need pleasure and sex is just a way to gratify that need. It is also required to give birth, thus life exists due to sex. Just like we learn to control our other senses, we should keep it under control too. Controlled sex is not bad and having it with a person you love becomes spiritual, as it is about making your partner feel loved, pampered and respected."

Anil admired her for her strength of character. They ordered for dinner at the room itself and continued to spend those leisurely moments together, until a phone call disrupted them. It was Nandita Di.

"Oh gosh!" Kavita's heart sank as if someone had knocked at their fantasy land. Though Nandita Di had called for a casual talk, Kavita felt a certain febrility. Her face got as pale as a fearful ewe. "What happened, dear?" Anil asked.

She was still in quivers. What a high speed our mind has! It changes itself within microseconds. The moments that had been filled with love, suddenly changed into those of fear and guilt. "For my own pleasure, I am lying to my family," she couldn't help tears brimming over her lashes.

Anil correlated the situation with the phone call and read her mind.

"Kavita, there is nothing wrong in doing so. It is just that we deserve our time together too and we cannot make them realize how badly we have been missing each other, that if we didn't work on it right away, we would soon have fallen into looking for someone outside the marriage. This situation is quite under our control. Tell me, what responsibilities have you left unfulfilled? You arranged for a tutor for them and a cook at home. You have always been their guiding force, a mentor and a great support to the family. Both of us have been longing for each other. Don't lose heart now, dear. We are not doing anything illegal or unethical. I love you."He hugged and kissed her.

It was not easy for her to get convinced. Though it had been her idea to hide it, she was unwilling to carry it out any further. She was also worried about the repercussions of getting caught. But then, in the name of respect and traditions, their relationship had been suffering and it was important to put some life back into it. She tried to justify the situation. At times, rationalization becomes really necessary to defend ourselves. After all, we need to believe our own explanations.

They enjoyed their companionship, releasing their stress and worries about the world. It was really amazing for them to be able to gather all those lost years into one single night. This was actually that quality time which they had badly been missing.

The next morning was quite a lazy one. His conference was scheduled only for a few hours during the day, so there wasn't much rush. They avoided making calls back home, but WhatsApp was a good alternative. After having breakfast, Anil got ready to go. He asked Kavita about her program for the day. She chirped, "I will be MYSELF today." He smiled, kept some money in her hand, gently kissed on her forehead and said, "Enjoy."

The natural proclivity of human beings is to enjoy in company, yet sometimes, self indulgence is pleasurable beyond measure. Generally, due to so many responsibilities and relationships, a bonding with our SELF is kept at stake. We tend to forget that relationships exist because the SELF exists. If there is no SELF, where will the relationships grow from? She knew that she had got a rarest of the rare opportunities to be with her own SELF and was determined to make the most of it. She hired a cab and left the hotel. The lady's day out with money in her hand and freedom in her heart, could not get any more thrilling.

But destiny had planned something even better for them. Kavita took a liking for a lovely scarf for Anil. She called him and asked if he could spare some time to have a look. She was at a market close to the conference venue, so it wasn't too difficult for Anil. While Kavita waited for him, she was noticed by someone, without her awareness.

"Yes! This is definitely Kavita *masi*." Scrolling down his engagement photographs, he finally managed to recognize her. It was Aayush. He was in Pune for a training program scheduled by his company. He noticed Kavita and tried to recall her appearance, as he wasn't so sure if she could actually be there. But as soon as he confirmed that it was her, he looked up and she was not there anymore.

By then, Anil had come and Kavita took him along for a final selection of the scarf. Aayush tried to locate her again and looked around in each shop. Anil was in a hurry, thus both of them left the place pretty soon. When they where boarding a cab, Aayush managed to get a glimpse of Kavita again, but missed the person that she was accompanied by.

With endless doubts and queries in his mind, he called up Saumya to confirm.

"Hi! Saumya, how are you?"

"Oh! Aayush, all well. You've called during working hours, what happened?" she asked, feeling a little strange, as Aayush usually called her up only late at night.

"Nothing urgent, dear. I just wanted to know whether Kavita masi is in Pune."

*How weird! Why was he asking about masi all of a sudden?*Saumya found it quite erratic. After a pause, she asked in return, "What happened? Why are you asking about her all of a sudden?"

"I think she is here and…and she is with someone."

That was a really shocking news for her to absorb. "I'll get right back to you," she told him.

She then enquired her mother about it and got to know that Kavita had gone for a family outing near her place. She decided not to reveal the shocking news to her mother, before she could really be sure about it.

Another shocking realization hit her when she logged on to Facebook and saw Tanay's status, which said: *Free bird! Mom with masi and Dad out for conference.*

'Aayush was right,' she thought. 'But it's impossible.' She could not bring herself to believe it.

Chapter 12

The Mystified Affair

They had a wonderful time. This out of the box feeling was preserved in their hearts forever. The positivity inside them was exhibited in their outward attitude too. They loved that surreal experience and the way it was moving. Despite all the responsibilities and shortage of time, they had been able to manage it. That feeling gave them the boost to live more lively. No one at home got to know about their secret, so things were pretty normal.

But life was not the usual for Saumya anymore. She was in a really bad state of mind since she had heard about Kavita's affair. That was something very unusual.She shared a beautiful bond with her *masi* due to the lesser age gap between them, but when you hear things like that about your loved ones, you tend to fall into denial. Though the evidence presented a far different story than what Saumya wanted to believe in. She really wanted to decode the mystery as soon as possible, but also found it difficult to stand in front of her *masi* and confront her. Another problem was that her would-be husband had formed a completely different image of the whole episode. Basically, she found herself in a soup.

At last she made up her mind to talk to Kavita first about the whole thing before framing any judgements in her mind. So, without revealing the half known facts to her mother, she decided to fly down to her*Masi*'s place. The shopping excuse made it easy for Saumya to convince her mom about her mood. Nandita di called up Kavita to inform her about Saumya's arrival.

"Wow! That will be so wonderful," Kavita exclaimed on the phone, oblivious to the fact that her secret was now known to Saumya.

Saumya had a terrible flight, as she had been undergoing a myriad of emotions altogether. In complete denial of all ill feelings towards Kavita, she reached on schedule. At her age, it was difficult to hide her emotions, but she managed it somehow. In fact, she could not find a single reason to doubt her masi's modesty. She had always considered Kavita as a perfect blend of all feminine qualities. She tried to collect all the pieces of the story to reach at the truth. Through her conversation with Tanay and Tanvi, she could easily make out that there was some ugly truth hidden beneath the surface. Naturally, *masu*'s Ahmedabad conference, *masi* being at her place, Aayush's truth, almost everything pointed towards a rather different story. Moreover she was disturbed about her masi's mutilated image in Aayush's mind.

Saumya was also afraid that revealing the truth would hamper some relationships forever. Thus, she just could not gather the courage to confront Kavita, with the fear of that self inflicted injury.

"Aayush, can we meet somewhere?" She finally called up Aayush to sort herself first. He had been looking forward to meet her but did not expect this to be the situation. They met in a garden and despite being a newly engaged couple, they looked like worried old guardians. It was difficult for Aayush to disclose this story to his parents too. It being an arranged relationship, the families were not so close that they would understand each other so well. Saumya slid off her ring and handed it over to Aayush.

"What's this?"he snapped.

"Please don't react, Aayush. I won't be able to see my family suffer such an embarrassment. I know it is equally embarrassing to break it off like this with you, but I have no other option. This probably is the best solution."

Aayush held her hands in his and suggested her to maintain her calm before drawing conclusions. "When I saw you for the first time, I knew that you were the one I had been looking for. This ring will only ever be yours, dear. I cannot leave you for someone else's immaturity." His understanding attitude touched her heart. The maturity with which he handled the situation ignited some feelings inside her. Being in an arranged arrangement, love happened at its own pace. Saumya could feel the inception of it happening.

Oh! The emotionally dramatic dilemma was too much to handle. Saumya told herself while sipping her cup of coffee with her *masi*. Everything was so beautiful. It was a cozy afternoon, sun-rays peeping inside the window with tea time *gup-shup and* crackling of groundnut peels. Why do we connect ourselves so deeply with others? If someone else is at fault, why do we punish ourselves for his/her mistakes? Why do we correlate the guilt from our relationship with that person? Why do we get so emotionally drained that we suddenly start perceiving a person in dark hues, without even giving them chance to reason out their actions? At times, our own jigsaw of unnecessary thoughts disturbs us and we expect others to jolt us out of it. Endless thoughts were disturbing Saumya while she pretended to be a part of the conversation with Kavita. Kavita was also busy talking about relationships, without noticing that Saumya was actually not wholly indulging with the chat. Many a times, Saumya felt the itch to ask Kavita about everything openly, but something was stopping her from doing so.

"Uh, what a horrendous situation! How can I just go and ask *masi* abruptly about it?" Saumya muttered to herself. She had to fly back home after two days and she was unable to settle down the maelstrom churning inside her.

This crisis situation, however, did have a positive aspect to it. Saumya had started to feel more secure with Aayush. That one week had given the two of them enough time and Saumya had started to develop some strong feelings for him. The love which had been undefined till then, finally found its true meaning. The blurred emotions came to focus in the form of some new emotions. Their immature minds had reached that state of accepting one another, irrespective of anything else. Maturity was on its way and it had probably begun to define the landmarks of their relationship.

It was another Friday evening and as a matter of routine,Kavita was in full zeal to engage in her secretive mingling.

"Mamma, I will go to Aparna's place this evening."

Krishna ji just nodded her head, as that had become a regular affair and there was nothing to discuss on it.

'Is *masi* actually going to meet her friend in the evening?' Saumya thought.

"Hi, Aayush. I think *masi* will be meeting him this evening. Can you help me out?"

"Any time, just tell *masi* that you want to accompany her and try to make some excuse for it, like you are getting bored, of something like that.Just make sure that she does not sense anything about you being aware of her Pune trip," Aayush guided her like a guardian.

"Don't worry, I will handle it. You just be ready when I call in the evening."

It was time to crack the puzzle at last. More than Kavita, Saumya was waiting for the dusk to arrive now.

Kavita chose to wear her her best outfit for that evening.Her body language made it quite clear that she was excited about the evening and had no tinge of doubt in her mind about Saumya's intentions. She was about to leave when Saumya unleashed her horses. "*Masi*, can I come along?"

'Oh! God, what should I do?' Kavita thought hard. She gulped her words down her throat and tried to escape, but that was not possible anymore. All of a sudden, an idea flashed through her mind.

"Why don't you call Aayush and ask him to meet you? It's your courtship time and it will never return, *meri jaan!*"Kavita praised herself wordlessly for her spontaneity in thinking of a way out, still unaware of the fact that this was exactly what Saumya had expected.

Saumya blushed and showed her affirmation for the idea. Kavita offered to drop her at Aayush's office on her way. Saumya called Aayush to check his preparedness towards executing their plan and also instructed him to be prompt so that they could follow Kavita.

Kavita dropped her off and carried on with her program to meet Anil. Lost in her own thoughts, she had not imagined even in her wildest thoughts that someone could be following her. It was a difficult situation for Saumya as well. She was dissecting her own thoughts left and right to solve the mysterious puzzle which had created such a thunder in her life.

Kavita and Anil met and got lost talking to each other, engrossed in themselves, without looking around. That was their time, where nothing could come in between them.

"Oh my God! Just look at them, Aayush. We lost our sleep because of them and here they are, enjoying their lives,"exclaimed Saumya, confronting the couple.

"So this was your plan this whole time, Saumya?" Kavita looked embarrassed.

"*Masi*, Aayush caught you in Pune."

"What? Where?" asked Kavita.

"At the shopping mall. I saw you waiting for someone," replied Aayush.

"Me, of course," Anil clarified.

"But why like this?" Saumya inquired with a shocked expression.

"Couple space," Kavita replied while looking at Anil. "You will understand it later."

"Aayush actually missed out *masu* in Pune and that status update by Tanay really confused us, so we had to do this sting operation and look, we had made a mountain out of a molehill. Oh! You can't even imagine the emotional turmoil I went through."

"Oh! My little doll has grown up. Thank you so much for keeping it a secret. I can't explain it dear, but let me be very clear with you, I love to live each moment with your *masu*."

"*Masu*! You are a true champ. You still rule her heart."

Anil held Kavita's hand in his and replied,

"Jab tod diye mohabbat ke usool humne

To phir zubaan ki ho aazmayish kaisi

Wo mere dil ka haal jaante hai

To bhala kehne sunne ki gunjaayish kaisi

Hai mere wajood mein shamil tera ehsaas

To phir paabandiyon ki paimaayish kaisi."

(We are breaking the rules of love, then why do we need to explain it to others. My love can read my heart, so there is no need to express it.She is the core of my existence, then why should we measure the restrictions on us.)

People around them loved to hear this new parameter of love. Everyone clapped. Saumya's eyes twinkled and were filled with pride for her *masi*. If she had carried the onus of her *masi*'s immorality she would never have come to know the truth behind it and feel good about her again. To her surprise, Kavita then spoke about the iceberg that tends to form between couples during the middle age, which, if not worked upon in time, can worsen the relationship. There were endless insights about this beautiful relationship called love, which cannot be bound by any relationship. Saumya flew back home with a promise to maintain their secret. She had also preserved some beautiful memories in her heart forever. The mystique that was carried by the expression of love, dwelled in her being.

Chapter 13

Getting New Wings

It came as a great surprise to her. She had been busy with the household chores, when her mobile rang.

'Who is that?' she thought while looking at the phone screen on which an unknown number was flashing. "Hello," she said, taking the call.

"Hello, am I talking to Kavita?" an unfamiliar voice responded.

"Speaking," she said, inquisitive to know what it was about.

"Hi Kavita, this is Abhinna Srivastava, Manager of The Samantha Group. I appreciate your eye for designing delicate jewellery. Can you please come for a meeting to discuss about making some new fashion jewellery in stone and pearl for our clients?"

Astound, she stammered, "W...what time?"

"Please check your mailbox. We will be sending the details of the meeting through mail."

She took some time to believe her words. Not ready to divulge this conversation at home, she eagerly waited for Anil to come back from work.

After dinner, she finished all her normal coarse jobs and went to her room. As always, Anil was watching news.

"You know Anil, I got a call from The Samantha Group today. They want me to design some jewellery pieces for their clients. I am really surprised. Where did they get my contact details from?" She looked at Anil to clarify her doubt about the possibility of Anil's involvement in it.

Anil muted his favourite channel to look at her and said, "Go for it, dear."

"I guessed it right. You are indeed behind it. At least you could have asked me. It had become too difficult for me to segregate my responsibilities anymore." She felt distraught.

"Through these years, you have given your all to make this house a home, without thinking twice about your own identity. In the last couple of days, since we started meeting outside, I have realized the need to rekindle our individual passions. I had always wished to join theatre, but destiny demanded something else from me. You had a passion to design jewellery. Then why do you want to waste your talent?Luckily, you have now got an opportunity to do it. Grab it. I am with you."

Anil's encouraging words were not enough still to convince her of it. "It demands a lot of commitment. How will I gather the strength to do everything so smoothly? I am really scared."

"If you are passionate about something, it will naturally drive you. You don't need any motivation to follow your passion. In fact, your passion drives you towards living completely. Think about the sense of fulfilment. You will make it, if you plan it properly. Trust me, you can do it," he went on.

"Your passion for your work defines the strength of your character. Any excuses towards that show your weakness. You are a role model to your children. They will definitely understand your commitments. You have always prioritized their upbringing above your own identity. It is time to cherish your upbringing along with your passion now. Once they grow up and get busy with their lives, the *what if's* will start coming back to you." She had tears flowing down her cheeks but carefully listened to everything he said. She tried to understand her husband's insightful words. Sometimes, love stays undefined in terms of parameters. When the bond between two different persons gives a single outcome, it becomes baseless to talk about separate identities. Their love had reached to another level. The bond that allows two people to share a common comfort zone is, perhaps, true love. She felt herself truly in love again.

"How did they come to know about it?" she asked him.

"When you gave me your laptop for security installation, I took it to office and while scrolling, I saw your jewellery portfolio on it. It was awesome. Initially, I thought I would ask you to design for our own clients but that would have attracted some obligatory issues at the office. So I mailed it to one of my contacts. It clicked and believe me, I have nothing to take credit for. You deserved it and so they chose you," Anil revealed the suspense.

She hugged him and they slept, content in their relationship.

The next day after all her morning chores, Kavita felt a strange kind of nervousness inside her, something like the feeling one gets before an exam. She shared it with Anil and asked him to help her hide the details of the happenings in her life. It was probably the fear of rejection which thoroughly forced her to execute things without telling anyone. Facing rejection at that age seemed like a huge embarrassment. In her heart of hearts, she never wanted to be answerable to either the children or her in-laws.

It was a formal meeting where they asked her to present a few samples before placing any purchase orders. On her way back, she directly went to the market to collect some ideas about what the present scenario was like. There were endless thought trains running in her mind regarding the designs she wanted to display as samples. It also demanded a lot of planning to manage things at her home front, along with this new responsibility that she wanted to adhere to. She wanted to match up to her best.

That week was a crucial time period for her. She felt as if she had been given new wings to fly. She wanted to soar high into the limitless sky, but was also scared to start. She tried to manage her time during the children's school hours, as at that time, she did not have enough to fill her basket. Krishna ji usually liked to spend that time with her social work and all Jagmohan ji wanted was to enjoy his solace with his soulful music. Thus, she could manage her sky to a certain extent, as far as time was concerned. Besides time, there was yet another constraint, her fear factor, to which Anil was all too familiar. His unconditional support helped her overcome her weaknesses. He always motivated her to be consistent in following her passion.

Finally the day arrived when she had to exhibit her designs. She had prepared almost 15 pieces, each one a unique piece of art. Anil admired her designs and wished her luck before leaving for work.

She struggled hard with her inner feelings and tried to look and behave normally, but her naïve and simple deportment actually helped her win all the hearts in a jiffy. Her designs truly defined her standard and the beauty of her character lay in her flexibility, which is usually missing in professionals these days. Finally, she was able to get orders on almost 8 of her designs, which was a great achievement in itself. She forced her emotions to take a backseat, at least till she came out of the office.

Life could not get better than this. She had tears in her eyes while she sat in her car. A stay at home parent is a job of big responsibility, which had instilled in her a never-say-die approach towards life. She had gained experience managing the varied outlooks at home, and she felt glad that her experience as a home maker had not all gone to waste. That day proved to her that she was not a completely inexperienced person, but had the attitude of making people willing to follow her. It was the most satisfying experience of her life. She cherished each moment with gratitude. With an overwhelming emotion of gratefulness, she called Anil and said, "Thank you for making me the luckiest woman on earth."

"So you got your first order?" Anil replied, happy and surprised. "This is just the beginning, my business woman. You've always had it. It is just that you had chosen me over it. Love you."

"They have given me a month's time to make fifty pieces of each design. I need some people to help me out. How will I execute it?"

"We'll find a way out. Don't worry." Like a mentor, he guided her.

Undoubtedly, life is never too short to achieve something. It was the first step, yet to take the first step at her age was the real challenge. She knew it was going to be impossible without her husband's support. Life was fair enough to return her dues. Not everyone in this world is lucky enough to get it. She felt indebted towards God. The next challenge was to execute it without revealing anything at home. She wanted to surprise her family by showing them that if the women staying at home could make their lives easy, then they can do wonders for themselves too. Apart from that, she still harboured doubts in her mind about the execution of her orders and feared that facing rejection or failure at that point of time could prove to be fatal for her startup plan. Beyond everything, she dreaded admitting failure in front of her loving family. Thus, all she wanted was to complete her first order without communicating about it with anyone at home.

Anil proved to be a big support in arranging a small place on rent for her. He encouraged her to give her passion her best. It is rather easy to do something you love, than doing what you don't love, so managing things was not that difficult. The biggest trouble, however, was to execute the order while concealing her own whereabouts for the next few days.

Chapter 14

Hide and Seek

New avenues were defined. Everything happened as per the consent of her destiny. Sometimes, certain things happen in our life without any planning at all. But this 'unplanned' is often much better than the 'planned'. We form a pattern of expectations when we plan something, but if things are directed presciently by destiny, there is no scope for expectations, as the unexpected naturally comes to you. This natural happiness fills one with a sense of gratitude. Kavita truly enjoyed this unexpected bliss. The affair with her husband could be such a wonderful experience, she had never imagined.

"Mamma, Aparna is looking for a new accommodation. She hardly knows anyone here so she has asked me to help her out. I am thinking of going along with her for the next couple of days while the children are at school." While making excuses in the name of Aparna, she kept her fingers crossed. She knew that it was easier to tell a make-believe story than to give a lame excuse everyday about her whereabouts for the next few days.

Moreover, Krishna ji's own women empowerment meetings were in session so she had no issues about anything till the time she was not asked to step out of her own comfort zone. Though she was not very happy with Kavita's out of the way involvement with her friend, yet being as she was, Krishna ji didn't unnecessarily involve herself in Kavita's personal life. Who doesn't want his/her own share of space after all? The ladies of the house were more comfortable giving that space to each other.

Kavita had already sorted out the household chores with the extra 'help' at home. Things were actually under control. She realised that it was not difficult at all to manage her work, with a little extra planning. It is rather easy to manage things when the schedule is tight, than to do the same when one has enough time. The new routine started soon and despite being busier than before, she strangely felt more energetic and enthusiastic. Her work gave her the most satisfying experience-the experience of fulfilment. Along with her team of four girls, she managed the production effectively.

Things at home had not changed much. The usual generational gap tiffs continued, but Kavita was now so engrossed in her busy schedule, so left those things to their fate. She tried to accept this bitter truth of her life and the guilt that followed hiding so many things from her family. Still playing hide and seek with her loved ones was somehow disturbing her. But then, who gets a plate full of sweets every time? She would often get into this futile exercise of justifying to her inner conscious the hiding of details from her supportive in-laws and such loving kids. Perhaps it was necessary, in order to not hurt anybody's sentiments. She could not help but confess her thoughts and emotions to Anil.

"Anil, it is really unfair on our part to keep them in the dark. I feel like I am ditching them."

"it's just a matter of a week, dear. As soon as your first order gets dispatched, we will tell him about it."

"it is not about that. It is about our mysterious affair."

"Kavita, look. Our children are growing up and our parents have reached the age where it is very difficult to make them understand certain things. Everything is perfectly placed. Then why do you want to create ripples unnecessarily? We have to maintain that 'decorum' in front of their eyes. Let the veil stay the way it is, but honestly, I don't want to lose out on this 'fun'. I have been missing it for so long."

She found herself entrapped in a situation where she was unwilling not only to escape, but also to be caught. She tried to be cohesive about the situation, but it was in vain. Though it was her own brainchild to start the affair with her husband, but she had never expected to be caught in the constraints of a self made web. Probably, she was scared of running the gauntlet. At the same time, she never wanted to leave the fairytale of her life.

The next day, she gathered up her courage to confront them with the truth and decided to finish off the hide and seek game once and for all. She was about to head out and reveal everything when she heard a loud scream.

"Tanay, will you please switch off that howling music?" That was Krishna ji's voice.

"Lemme enjoy, *dadi*."

The two of them got into their usual spat again. Kavita tried to cool down the situation unwillingly, but it was such a big task to reconcile things between them. Both had their own valid opinions and wanted to justify their own points above the other. Choosing one side between them meant inviting even more trouble, so she chose the middle way and somehow managed to reduce the heat. In the meantime, however, her courage to reveal the truth got subdued. She always tried to be placid in such pitiless situations, but as a human being she expected some grace. There was a mutiny of thoughts in her mind.

"Fraud! It's a fraud," she muttered as she sunk deep into her challenging zone. "Isn't life too pre-determined in terms of living? Are we really enjoying it? Always busy with so many schedules, time always seems to be pre-arranged for the next job. We are simply headed towards some undefined goal with undetermined strengths and endless weaknesses. Our life is poles apart from the imaginative world, the world of a small child's fantasy, still reluctant to enter the domain of grown-ups, unwilling to leave its comfort zone, wishing to enjoy each bit of it. But no…life is something else. It is about taking responsibilities, fulfilling the demands of others without any expectations in return. This one sided duty cannot demand any credit, and if credit is demanded, you are labeled as selfish'. Above all that, the judgmental attitude of the society locks us in the strange role of a misfit. Oh! How I wish I could bluff my life just once. And when destiny has given me the chance ,do I really want to forego it? No!"It was crystal clear in her mind now that she would keep her secretive affair a secret only. "After all, freedom is each individual's birthright. So what, if we need to steal it from our own life?"

She dialed Anil's number. "Hi! Anil, can we go out for a movie today?"

That was an unusual demand for Anil during his office hours. While sitting in a meeting, he could only tell her that he would call her back in some time. This 'some time' of these husbands can never be defined. She knew that it was not fair to assume that Anil was not willing to understand her state of mind, but probably was genuinely busy. However, she was totally unwilling to follow any protocols. In that frame of mind, she went out for a walk. "If only we could have a recess in our life too." She was still in her rebel mood, pining for her inner freedom. She wanted to feel that bondage free life on her own. She wandered around purposelessly for a few moments and tried to assimilate the beautiful evening in her mind, along with the fluttering sound of wings and the nature retiring to a moon-lit sight. Then, she went to sit on a bench in a garden, realizing the need to restore the serenity of her mind. Sometimes, this inner peace requires to reconnect with reality.

She hadn't realized when her phone got switched off. When she switched it on, it rang, pulling her back to her old world.

"Your phone had been switched off for so long, Kavita. Where are you?"

"I am playing hide and seek with my life."

The concerned husband smiled and replied, "Let's play together."

Kavita went back home. This was probably the first time that she had behaved in such an irresponsible manner. Anil just ordered food from outside as nothing had been prepared at home. Krishna ji didn't question it, yet she was not very comfortable with this attitude. The muteness on the dining table reflected that something had gone terribly wrong that day. Kavita looked at Anil and he blinked at her, expressing his unconditional support for her. The inner conflict finally settled down, leaving something unsettled in the situation.

Chapter 15

The Well-Spun Tale

Anil knew that it was time to adjure his life to go on at his own terms. Till when could he remain a mere puppet, acting by the so called rules of the society. He wanted that spicy romance to escalate even more and to celebrate it with the love of his life, without any vindication.

However, there was a clear sign of unacceptability regarding Kavita's awry behaviour at home. Kavita herself was ashamed of not being herself the previous evening. The society, after all, expects decency from a mother of two teenagers. She had never shown scorn for any of her responsibilities before, but it was probably the girl in her who wanted to leave the shell of being responsible at all times. She was a grown adult, well into her thirties, so what?

Many events had happened back to back that received dissent at home. Others were hardly affected, but Krishna ji was not willing to digest the change. Despite being in a flustered state, she was willing to clear the matter without anymore delay. Kavita, on the other side, wanted to avoid any such confrontation because of her own reasons. A typical *saas bahu* episode commenced in the house. Everyone else lacked the vigour to engage in the situations at home. It did, however, put a rest to the fierce clashes between the two distant generations.

Despite all cautions, the serious confrontation happened on the same morning that Kavita had to deliver her final assignment.

"Are you her only friend available in the whole city? Why don't you open up a help centre of your own?" Krishna ji said quite rudely.

Well prepared for such a comment, Kavita calmly replied,

"Mamma, it is just a matter of a few days. How can I just tell her to manage things on her own at this point?"

"Why? Is she unmarried?"

"No! She is separated."

"Oh! But, why? Do you think she will remain loyal to you, if she doesn't even know how to handle a relationship? You should maintain your distance with her."

"Mamma, things don't always move the way we expect them to. It doesn't have to do with loyalty every time. At times, it is about your own space. Anyway, I'll keep it in mind."

"Okay, but take care, beta." Krishna ji never wanted to make a big deal out of a trivial issue, yet it had started. She wanted to talk about the sudden change in her behaviour, but when things started to take an ugly turn, she handled it with care. She always gave precedence to relationships over arguments.

Kavita was well aware of the situation and felt really good about Krishna ji's way of handling things maturely, but she wondered at the same time as to what happens to this wonderful person when her opponent is Tanay.

She breathed a deep sigh and left the house.

This was the final countdown. She entered the office to submit her consignment. She was asked to collect her cheque from the accounts department. It was a small amount, but the feeling she got was unfathomable. She clicked a photograph of her first cheque and sent it to Anil. While sitting in her car, she called him up enthusiastically. Enraptured by her sense of achievement, she exclaimed, "Let's celebrate, Anil!"

"Hold on, Kavita. Okay, fine. Let's go for a movie together. Then we will dine out."

Kavita laughed to her heart's content and remarked, "MOVIE!" Do you even remember the last time we went to a movie together?"

THE FLASHBACK

Kavita was busy frying *pakoras* for the family, when Anil entered and declared the movie plan. Within no time, everyone was ready to move. Anil had booked only two tickets but could not reveal it to the family. He went to the toilet to book more tickets and just to show that he had booked all the tickets together, he rebooked the two tickets again. Finally, the previous booking could not be cancelled and the money spent on them ended up getting wasted.

This episode was still a teasing tickle between them and Kavita's sarcastic remark instigated that episode to come over the surface again. He took it as a challenge and chuckled, "*Agge agge wekhiye, hondda hai ki* (Wait and watch what happens next)."

In the evening, at the dining table, Anil spun a tale.

"Mamma, one of my friends is having trouble in his marriage. I'm thinking of visiting him. I've told Kavita to be ready tomorrow evening."

There was no point of discussion beyond that, though Krishna ji kept enquiring about the details of that fake story and Kavita giggled in her heart of hearts.

When certain things follow a change, it is not always difficult to accept them, but a fixed mind set has its own boundations. Up to an extent, everyone is cogent in his/her own mindset, but when it comes to 'adapting to another's change', it truly becomes a difficult job and it is important then to make guarded effort, so that no one ends up feeling hurt. The Indian *saas-bahu* culture is also the same. The initial stages of this relationship are bound to suffer a rift, but in due course of time, the blend of this relationship become essential for the well being of the home.

It was not that Krishna ji had never been a hinderance to their independence before, but over a period of time, everyone had become habitual of adjusting with each other. The concept of individual space, however, had not been clearly understood, making some things inexplicable and silent, just to avoid unnecessary disturbances. The sudden change in Kavita's behaviour naturally brought about a friction. Change is always resisted before it is accepted. Kavita took that resistance positively and enjoyed the flow of the change. Krishna ji was still in a dazed situation as she could smell something cooking, but could not find where the '*khichdi*' was.

Chapter 16

Teens and Grands

Tanay planned to go out for a movie with his friends. He cooked up the excuse of group study at home to conceal his whereabouts. Coincidentally, both he and Kavita reached the ticket counter at the same time. Tanay was lucky enough to escape from being caught as he had spotted his mother from a distance, and before Kavita could notice him, he conveniently vanished.

'Mom, here?'he thought surprised, but in his fear and distress of getting caught, he did not pay much attention to what his mom could be doing there. He actually felt relieved for having made the narrow escape. "Who wants unnecessary arguments about who is right, parents or teens? And then the thumb-rule follows,'You are not big enough to argue with your parents. You are not mature enough to take charge of your life. We are your parents and we know what is good or bad for you, blah blah blah,' and all such centuries old lectures by parents which they consider their birthright to nag us," Tanay thought. The teen's brain was turning rebellious to find his own space.

Teenage - the one time in one's life where one can take as many chances as one wants, to explore the unexposed, to challenge the unexplored. Tanay was growing up and was undergoing many bodily changes along with changes in his perception. After all, he had his own individual identity now with his own developing thought process. Things which remained unexplained by the parents, sought different sources and perspectives to make sense to kids this age. He was also perhaps mesmerised by splendid vision of the new world around him. Adventurous and raunchy, looking for a thrilling and electric life, he was only trying to explore the world around him, at the cost of lying to his parents.

On his way back home, he cancelled his program for going to the movie. He was more happy about his escape, regardless of his plan getting spoiled in the process. It was quite natural for him to rely more on his friends than his family. He settled down sooner with the tuitions at home, without thinking much about what had happened at noon that day.

After the tuitions got over, Kavita declared a pizza party for that night.

"Anything special, mom?" the children enquired.

"Well, that's a surprise," she tried to hide her excitement.

Everyone waited for the curtains to draw.

The pizza soon got delivered and both Tanay and Tanvi bounced on it to grab the largest piece. They were ready to enjoy the delectable taste of the first bite when Kavita finally revealed, "I just finished a jewellery designing assignment for a company."

"Oh! That's awesome," Anil expressed his validation.

Krishna ji was perhaps not very happy.

"You could have told me about it before," Krishna ji expressed her resentment.

"I was actually skeptical about my success myself, so I wanted to give it a try without telling anyone."

"Whatever, Kavita. I have never stopped you for doing anything. I am really hurt," Krishna ji said, finally letting out the words she had been carrying in her heart.

Some thumb-rules always stay, perhaps. Be it at any age, parents are always parents. The last line for all mothers or mothers-in-law remains the same. "Do whatever you want, who am I to stop you?"

Kavita felt jitters run through her body and thought,'Oh my God! If this little secret is facing such scrutiny, what will their reaction be when they find out about our secret affair. Perhaps it's not correct to enjoy life on our own terms. We should have taken them into confidence." Kavita was filled with that haunting guilt factor once again.

"*Manu,tera hua ab mera kya hoga,*" Jagmohan ji enjoyed his pizza slice with Kishore Da's songs.

How apt those words were according to the situation!

With three different generations, with different needs and mindsets, under a single roof, clash were inevitable.

The teens wished to live as free birds. Life was pretty 'cool' for them. They believe in momentary pleasures. The pressures on them were enormous too, be it related to results or from their peers. They felt that no one ever understood them. Despite their body issues, game performances, the newly exposed world, the burning fire and the expectations, they tried to make their life cool by dancing and singing it all out with loud music. But, was it that easy? A stressed life interspersed with playful moods, but everything comes at a cost, you see. They had to bargain for their space from the elders. All reward for them was based on good behaviour and performance. Moreover, because of the grandparents, they were always expected to adjust, which was not entirely fair.

As for the grandparents, they were not living too cool a life either, despite the contrary opinion. They have their own pattern of thoughts, shaped over a period of time. They are done with all kinds of noise and chaos, and only want to live out their retired age in peace. Relieved of their share of responsibilities, all they want is rest. They also have their own set of expectations and assumptions regarding the children and grandchildren. They too undergo stress due to body issues and ego synchronization problems. They love light music and are generally in a pray-full mood.

The major difficulty existed for the middle string, Kavita and Anil, who always found themselves busy trying to strike a balance between the playful and pray-full moods of the people in their house. More than that, they loved everything in moderation and their needs were never understood. The teens were unwilling to listen to them and the grandparents, unwilling to accept. Stuck in between such a mismatch, was their 'secret affair'.

Sometimes, life comes up with its own set of problems and at times, it gets messed up. Kavita was lost in thought again on how to clear up the mess in her life?

Chapter 17

The Cross-Check

Tanay told Tanvi about having seen their mom at the ticket counter, but didn't mention what he had been doing there himself. Tanvi, being her dadi's favourite, spoke to her about it. It was not a big deal, but since Kavita had been telling Krishna ji everything honestly lately, this unusual change disturbed her. She took it quite offensively that Kavita had started hiding things from her.

On the other hand, Anil felt himself quite influenced by the creative nature of the movie he had gone to watch with Kavita and was all praises while walking out of the multiplex. 'It is really amazing to watch movies of such different genres these days. The Directors are really opening up their minds to the audience,' he thought.

"The narration, the screenplay, the dialogue delivery, and most of all, the content was so amazing, I felt completely awestruck! Didn't you, Kavita?" he exclaimed.

Kavita appreciated the movie too, though she had enjoyed the company more. She was really happy to finally see Anil get out of his shell and seek his real inner self.

"Kavita, you know I have always wanted to get into this creative field. I have always wanted to pen down my imagination and live my characters. I have always wanted to direct my characters in such a manner that it leaves real impact on lives," he said, getting lost in his imagination.

"Anil....Anil," Kavita nudged him back to reality.

"At times, we don't realize exactly what our bent of mind really is," Anil said, taking a deep sigh which expressed his resentment and helplessness for not being able to follow his passion.

"Hun, are you not happy with your life?" Kavita asked, looking at him with a surrendered expression.

He read her expression and answered smilingly, "I love you, sweetheart. You are the one whom I love to see sleeping contently by my side and standing by me at all times as my support." Both of them looked into each other's eyes without realizing that they had been sitting inside their car in the parking area of the mall for a long time.

Overall, it had been a nice evening.

At the dining table the next morning, Krishna ji enquired about the fake friend that Anil had created. Anil cooked up a believable infidelity story of this so called friend and how they were filing for a divorce and all.

Anil then left for his work, informing them about some late night party at the hotel. Almost twice or thrice a week, Anil would come home late at night. Everyone was habitual of that routine. Krishna ji was actually quite displeased with Kavita's behavior and wanted to express her views on the same to her.

Kavita had some work at the bank however, so she soon left too.

A little while after she left, the door bell rang.

Claccy aunty opened the door.

"Is this Kavita's house?" a lady asked.

"*Memsaab ghar pe nhi hai* (Madam is not at home)," Claccy replied casually.

"Who's there?" Krishna ji asked while walking towards the main door.

"Hello Auntie, I am Aparna, Kavita's friend. It had been quite some time since I last saw her, so I thought of visiting to surprise her."

All hell broke loose in Krishna ji's mind. It took her a bit of time to bear the hit.

"Oh, come inside!" Krishna ji spoke, recovering from the shock. Instinctively she asked, "When did you meet her last?"

"Two months back, auntie. At a coffee shop. I guess she called you up while she was with me."

"Oh! Yes, I remember."

Aparna was completely unaware of what she had done. She just went on, "I misplaced my phone and all my data was saved in that phone. I had a vague idea of the address, so I am here. Your neighbours directed me to your house. When is she back? Can I have her contact no?"

"No," Krishna ji replied spontaneously. She soon took a grasp on her emotions and tried to be normal. "Oh, yes! Her number. Let me check on my phone. Memorizing phone numbers is so out of fashion these days. These smartphones keep our memories at rest," she remarked.

Aparna shyly smiled.

Krishna ji gave her the phone number and purposely replaced one digit, so that Aparna would not be able to contact Kavita and inform her about their meeting. She wanted to find out all that had been going on right under her nose.

"Have some tea. Actually, Kavita might take some time to come back,"Krishna ji offered as a gesture.

"Oh! Thanks, auntie. Actually, I am going abroad for an office assignment. I will be leaving this Sunday. If possible, I will call her up and plan something before that.If not, then I will only be able to meet her after two months. I should leave now. Thanks for the number, auntie," Aparna told her before leaving.

As soon as Claccy closed the door behind her, the phone bell rang. She picked up the cordless and handed it to Krishna ji. "Memsaab, phone."

In her brain, multiple trumpets had started blaring. She received the call, still lost in thought, and said, "H..hello, who is there?"

"Namaste Auntie, Nandita this side. How are you?"

Krishna ji took a while to come out of the shock she had received just a few moments back.

"Yeah Nandita, how are you?"

"Auntie, is everything alright?"

Krishna ji was already apprehensive about something unusual going on around her in the house. Yet, she was also well experienced in hiding away the '*ghar ki baat*' from outsiders. It is quite natural that when you trust someone completely, you don't question them at all, but when even a little doubt about them takes root in your mind, not a single trace can be left unattended.

She was wise enough to understand that Kavita never went to Nandita's house and had lied about that too. This revelation from Nandita broke something inside her. She felt terrified of what lied behind these correlating circumstances. Within seconds, she tried to put together the recent happenings from the past and framed in her head all the jumbled pieces of the jigsaw together. Before drawing any conclusions, however, she wanted to dig deeper into this half baked story.

All said and done, that was definitely a topsy-turvy situation for her that took away her night's sleep.

Chapter 18

The Master Mind

The glaring reality of the situation made Krishna ji very submissive. She became unusually quiet and got confined within her own self. That morning was different and everyone noticed this change. She was a very strong lady and never tried to trigger unnecessary disturbances based on half known facts, yet she knew that the situation required stealthy action, for which there had to be strength in the house. Moreover, she never wanted things to take an ugly turn, on account of being dealt with in a haste. Above all, she believed in response more than reaction.

After a lot of brainstorming, she decided to make the teens her allies. She assessed the situation as being a critical one and worked towards uniting the family to deal with it. The first person to be taken into her confidence was obviously Jagmohan ji. Then, she secretively shared the half known facts with the children. Obviously, she was cautious enough to talk to them about it in a reserved way, so as not to put a wrong impression in their minds. She calmed them down by telling them not to jump to any conclusions before they dug out the complete truth. For that, they had to arrive at a consensus.

The next morning, everybody witnessed a lovely coordination between the distant generations. There was no argument between Tanay and Dadi. Dadu listened quietly to a new soothing song that Tanvi played. They even made a plan to go shopping together in the evening. Much to Kavita's surprise, they even executed the plan. She was really enjoying this newfound warmth and congeniality between the two generations. After coming back from the market, they showed her all that they had purchased. She really enjoyed this snugness between them.

At night, she told Anil all about it.

"Have you tried to figure it out?" Anil asked her surprised.

"Figure out what, Anil?" she asked.

"Their strange coordination, obviously. There is something fishy about it," remarked Anil.

"Be it anything, yaar. I am just so pleased to see it and feel it," she chirped enthusiastically.

Anil smelt something peculiar in all of it, but was happy to see Kavita feeling so good.

Things at home had suddenly started to function smoothly. Tanay's wildest tantrums were being accepted easily, as if the rule book had changed overnight. Their rigidity was replaced with flexibility. The two generations adapted to each others' needs without resistance. Kavita was happily surprised to see them accepting and confirming to each other.

Sunday, the usually 'not so cool' day, was strangely amazing too. No demands about specific breakfasts were made to Kavita. In fact, Dadu prepared French toasts for the kids, and everyone enjoyed the warmth of the house.

Anil noticed a strange eye contact between Krishna ji and Tanay.

"Papa, why don't you plan for a movie with mamma. It's been a long time since you took her out anywhere," Tanay said in a complaining tone.

Anil was about to sip his tea, but the cup almost slipped from his hand. Controlling himself, he looked up to reply, but before he could start, dadi spoke, "Right, Anil. Both of you don't go anywhere. You must take some time out for her."

Gasping in astonishment, Kavita and Anil looked at each other. Had they been caught?This was the first question that entered their minds.

"Oh God!" Kavita found it too difficult to face everyone.

Both of them found themselves short of words. They just went on listening to all the sermons being issued in their interest. They wanted to admit their uncanny affair, but were caught in deep embarrassment. The circumstances had left them in a strange situation, where it was equally difficult to both repudiate or validate their affair.

"Okay, movie, outing, dating, dinner," Anil blabbered on without thinking.

Kavita could relate to his muzzled state of mind and offered, "Let's have a chaat party tonight. What say?"

"That's a great idea," said Jagmohan ji. "Beta, order some pizza also."

"Hurray!" the kids exclaimed. Dadu never liked to have pizza usually.

Kavita and Anil found themselves dazed by such exceptional behavior at home. They could not freely talk about it in front of everyone, so they waited for everyone to turn in.

After dinner, everybody went into their respective rooms.

"Anil, I think you were right. There is something strange going on," Kavita spoke worriedly.

This time, Anil found himself feeling quite uncomfortable with regard to the revelation too.

"I think I should go and explain everything to Mamma. But Kavita, do you really think they know about it?" Anil asked, still feeling suspicious.

"Haven't you noticed a change in their body language? They must have noticed something, that's why they want to give us our space." Kavita felt really annoyed about the situation.

They wanted some space for themselves and it was being granted to them too, but they did not like the way things were unfolding. They felt like culprits at that moment. Anil went out to confess everything to his mother. He walked over to her room with heavy steps. However, when he reached her door, he heard some whispers coming out of her room. He peeped inside and was shocked to see the children and grandparents sitting together and discussing something. He alerted his senses to understand what was happening in there.

"Did you check when this NEEL is coming to meet her again?" Krishna ji asked Tanay.

"It's on Friday, dadi," Tanay said.

"Thank God that Kavita was not here when Aparna had come to see her. I just hope your papa really takes her out for the movie this Friday. Then we will go and find out who this person is. Ah! We ourselves are the reason behind this. We always think only about our own wishes. Your father hasn't been paying attention to her either. If only we had given her some space and some good time," Krishna ji said, taking a deep sigh.

Anil could sense the pain in his mother's voice.

"Don't worry, dadi. Mom loves us more than anything else. We will surely get her back," Tanay said.

"Good night, *bachhon*. Sleep well. We will work it out together, I am sure. Don't you two let your studies get affected due to this," dadi said.

"Good night, dadi. Good night, dadu." The children hugged their grandparents and made their way towards their own room.

While the children were coming out, Anil hurriedly trotted down to his own room.

A great sense of relief settled in his mind. For a moment, he had wanted to confess everything to his loved ones, but then he refrained. Never before had he experienced such a lovely bond between the members of his family. It was unimaginably surreal for him and all he wanted to do was to enjoy it a little further. He entered back into his room with a mischievous expression on his face.

Chapter 19

The Hidden Treasure

Kavita was ice cold when Anil touched her. Freezing with stress, she imputed her husband's touch to be highly confusing. With all varied expressions on her face, she looked at his mischievous look and asked, "What happened?"

With a heartfelt laughter he hugged her tightly and looked into her eyes with affection. She was unable to understand anything and her eyes constantly pleaded, "Damn it, just tell me."

"Relax, *jaaneman.*" He finally revealed the suspense without loosening his arms around her. "You are caught, I'm not."

Kavita got anxiously desperate to know what Anil really meant.

"Can you please open up properly? I'm skipping my heartbeat here and you find it thrilling," she expressed her discomfort.

Anil squeezed her in an attempt to soothe her and then said lovingly, "My dear lovely wife, what I saw today was unbelievable. They have a completely different story in their minds."

Kavita's expression changed in accordance with Anil's style of describing the whole sequence.

"They think that you are having an affair with some'NEEL'.No one has yet figured out that I am that Neel. They believe that you are the victim of everyone's careless behavior at home. They think that even I have failed to look after your basic needs and that you are actually disturbed due to the daily fights at home. So my dear, they think that they have lost you. All that coordination between them that you saw today is nothing but their attempt to bring you back into their lives," Anil explained.

All blood drained out of her face as she grew pale. She felt completely lifeless for some moments. Anil nudged her back to life and kissed her all over smilingly. She was as calm as a free flowing river on the outside, but with a storm raging below the surface. She succumbed to the demands of her husband as her brain had stopped working at that time. She lay bare in his arms and then spoke out her feelings to him.

"Anil, I feel naked in front of my family. Why didn't you tell them the truth? You are enjoying it while I am dying here with guilt," she broke down.

Anil hugged her tight and asked her, "Dear, do you know who planned this super coordination?"

She raised her brows expressing her curiosity.

"Tanay and mamma," Anil replied.

"Come again. Are you serious?" Kavita's eyes were wide open in surprise.

"You heard it right, sweetheart. Have some patience. Let's enjoy it and take it to another level. They feel themselves to be the culprits. I think you should let them feel that way till they actually realize that every individual needs some space and dignity to survive and that they should not have taken you for granted. I know it's the harder way to learn, but it is fine. At times, it is important to make people realize your worth. We will be more cautious about our affair now, but let the game be on. Everything come at a cost dear. If this is the cost of our affair, then let's enjoy the best of both worlds," Anil tried to pacify her.

Kavita somehow got convinced with his logic but was still not very happy with regard to showing such disparaging behavior towards her loved ones. After all, it is not easy to offend your own SELF, especially when you know you are right. "Ah! Being nostalgic to spend time with your partner is not so easy," she sighed and looked at Anil, who was in a peaceful sleep already.

"Let me take another chance if Anil is so sure about it. May be, it will unveil the hidden treasure of love within the family," she thought and closed her eyes to struggle with her sleep.

The next morning, the drama continued. Tanay gave dadi a hug before going to school. Dadu was dressed in his track suit instead of the usual kurta pyjama. All of this was perfectly planned. Though the makeover was cooked up, it was not intentioned to make anyone feel bad. Everything was pitched perfectly to make up a loving family. Anil smiled over it, while Kavita was still in shock. She could then correlate with what Anil wanted to say. He was right in taking some more time before telling the truth to their loved ones so that this so called crisis situation could smoothen out the friction between the two generations.

It was really a big thing for Kavita that her family was taking such a bitter pill with so much courage. They were working their fingers to the bone just to get her back in their lives. Despite the evidence of her involvement in some dishonourable activity in front of them, her mom-in-law blamed her own self instead of cursing her. Undoubtedly however, the deal was not that bad. They just had to continue misleading their loved ones to make them realize the importance of love in their life. Kavita was filled with gratitude towards such a loving family and was actually surprised at how a mysterious affair with her husband, brought out something that she had only dreamt of before. She got rather carried away by such beautiful love – the true essence of it. She felt indebted towards her destiny for giving her such a considerate family. What more could a person ask for? "A nice house, a lovely family and true satisfaction."

Undoubtedly, such changes are always welcome. Anil loved this changed family environment and enjoyed the situational makeover. Quite some things were still camouflaged and he wanted to see them changing into reality. He was happy that they had chosen to not suppress their emotions and the best part was that everyone was willing to impress one another. He knew that if the reality of the situation was made known to them, all arrows would then turn to their direction. All he wanted for the moment was for the suspense to live on a little longer, till his loved ones actually felt the heat.

The drama went on at both sides. Krishna ji was oblivious to the fact that Anil knew about their plan. Anil wanted to aggravate the ungainly thoughts in their minds to spark up the hidden love in his family. He could see that amazing coordination between the two most cross-natured people in his life, his mother and his son. He wanted to take full advantage of this situation to break the rebellious streak between them. While sitting in his office and sipping coffee, he scripted the entire drama to be played out over the next few days. He knew he was about to drag everyone into it, but it was for a good cause after all.

Kavita had not imagined that their private jingle would reach upto this extent. They had just wished to break away from the stagnation that had seeped into their lives. They had just wanted to refresh their imagination and relive some lost moments. But things had unexpectedly taken an ugly turn. "What more, now?" she asked herself.

A message pinged on her phone.

"When life seems to be astir,

Just go with the flow."

It was Anil. 'Oh! I guess he is also thinking of ways to get out of this problem. Or perhaps he has already found a way out of it,' she thought, unaware of the fact that she was about to become a part of the drama directed by Anil. Back at office, Anil smiled thinking about the surprises and shocks that he had planned to unveil. The Shakespeare in his mind said, "All's well that ends well."

Chapter 20

The Valid Argument

"NEEL, who is Neel?" This was the biggest question in her mind. "We will surely crack this puzzle today," Krishna ji told herself. There was something special about that Friday. Kavita had her usual plan to go out that evening. As soon as she told Krishna ji about her plan, Anil entered the house. Everyone was playing a role in that elaborate drama. Krishna ji insisted that Anil should take her out. Kavita made a face, showing her displeasure with the change of plans. This was all a part of the script that Anil had prepared.

Kavita and Anil went for their usual outing, planned unusually however, by none other than Krishna ji herself. As they moved out, the detective army was called to action. They left for their pre-planned destination, the coffee shop. They were completely prepared to finally find out what was happening in Kavita's life. They reached their destination without realizing that they were being followed by someone else. Anil and Kavita, obviously.

The grandparents and the grandchildren got engrossed in locating a solo person at the coffee shop, but it was in vain. Then the detective dadi showed Kavita's photograph to the waiter and asked him, "Have you seen her before?"

"Yes! She comes here every Friday with a man. They sit here for long hours and give a good tip to me as well. I don't know why they have not turned up here today," the waiter innocently replied.

"Can you click that man's photograph the next time they're here and send it on this number?" Dadi asked, giving Jagmohan ji's number to him.

"Very smart, dadi," Tanvi said.

Krishna ji looked at Tanay, who had turned as pale as a dove. She could easily read the teenager's mind. She ordered for some brownies for the children and tried to cheer him up.

"Tanay, you are not as rude as you seem to be."

Tanay looked at her with lots of admiration, but it was weird for him to peep into his mother's life like that.

The experienced and calm lady gave him a gentle pat on his back, in an attempt to give him some solace. She sipped her tea casually, but Tanay's faith was shaken.

Hiding behind the scene, Kavita could also read her son's emotions from a distance. Anil sniggered while looking at them on their detective spree, but Kavita felt like being swallowed whole by the ground, looking at her teenage children. She could see that paleness on Tanay's face. Tanvi was not in a good mood either. Kavita couldn't stand it any longer and walked away in another direction, Anil followed behind her. They took their seats in their car and Kavita finally expressed her fear to him.

"Oh! Anil, this is getting really difficult. I can't face this. How will they cope with this unnecessary stress?" she said, feeling disheartened.

"Don't worry, Kavita. Everything will be fine. Just enjoy it. They can handle it and this is not unnecessary, dear. You know it better than me. It is just the harder way to make them realize that good things happen to blessed people and that they need to appreciate what they have." Anil was quiet confident about his crafted tale and was well prepared for the twist he had planned.

The innate nature of a woman is different from that of a man. Women love to go deep into their relationships and are aware of the tenderness each relation seeks, so it was naturally difficult for Kavita to accept everything that was going around. They had definitely surpassed the stiffness between the two of them, but she was not willing to put her children's sentiments at stake for the sake of her own leisure. She felt a discord with regard to the story of disgrace rumoured against her. On top of all that, Anil was actually enjoying it.

It was a valid point of argument and both Kavita and Anil had different viewpoints on it. He went on telling Kavita to enjoy the situation and to look at the rumour in a positive way, but it was not so easy for her. Anil knew why he wanted to continue with it in that manner, but was unable to convince Kavita about it. He perceived that situation as a possible means of getting the two high headed generations together. He tried to give her his piece of mind by saying that the situation had posed a test in front of his mother and his son. As for Tanay it was a situational setback that could turn into a learning experience and for Krishna ji, it was the ideal situation to prove her views on women liberalization. Kavita knew that Anil was right to a certain extent, yet she could not dare put her son to such a test. Ah! mothers will always be mothers, and the mother in Kavita was not ready to give in. Married life is a blend of all hues and a mix of all spices.

"Sometimes black and white, while sometimes colour.

Sometimes sweet and sour, while sometimes bitter.

Sometimes utter or mutter, while sometimes butter butter."

"Had you been in my shoes, you would have realized how difficult it is. Imagine, if they start thinking about your illicit behavior instead of mine, what would you do then?" she said in a flustered manner.

"And if that happens, will you continue?" Anil looked into her eyes.

"Are you joking?" she felt taken aback.

"Don't worry. The game plan is ready. I will prove to them that it was because of my extramarital affair that you started yours. Please don't ask any further questions. I will let you know in some time." Anil tried to calm her down.

He started again, "I believe in your strength. Trust me, I'll not let things go over to the bitter side. We can't just let go of such a lovely chance to build a strong support system within the family. Even if certain things are not happening in the right way, you should understand that some things come at a cost. You can't expect life to be perfect every time. It is full of imperfections, but they lead us on to perfection. Deep inside every individual, there lives a child who wishes to live life unconditionally, yet in a guarded way. Every individual has the right to keep that child alive because if that child dies, you become dull. We have nurtured that child in us for so long. Why should we now accept that old sedentary lifestyle again, just because of some social boundations? Let's just live our life as it was meant to be lived, dear, instead of dying each day."

Kavita kept staring at Anil without blinking and could not argue against him any more. Anil's articulation of his thoughts relaxed her and was successful in convincing her. She believed in her own mettle and in Anil's love for her. She made up her mind to accept the situation and take another chance from destiny to accept love as the basis of her existence. In the very core of her heart, she let her instincts guide her further.

At last, she was prepared to play her role as scripted by Anil.

Chapter 21

Another Twist

A late night event was scheduled outside the hotel premises to which Anil was required to go. He used the opportunity fully to initiate his plan. Due to safety reasons, he offered Rakshanda to accompany him in his car. He planned it in such a manner that they would be alone in his car all the way to the venue. After picking her up from her place, he drove to his house and made a call to Jagmohan ji to tell him to come out for a moment. When Jagmohan ji came out, Anil stepped out of the car and handed over his laptop to him. Then, he went over to Rakshanda's window and leaned down to tell her something, on purpose. After this, he walked back to his seat and carried on. It was but obvious for anyone looking to have questions sprout in one's mind. Also, Jagmohan ji was the weakest string in the family that could easily be pulled.

Jagmohan ji recalled Anil's expression from that instance over and over again, trying to understand the situation and he felt the same each time. Undoubtedly, the nature of hospitality industry is such that it carries the risk of getting lured towards the opposite sex, but Anil's had always used this to boost his self control. However, this time he completely utilized this perception of his job to tarnish his own image. It didn't require much effort. Kavita knew what her husband had planned. Anil had also mentioned to the front desk at his hotel that he was going back home. He knew that after a doubt had crept into his father's mind, he would definitely enquire about it at his office. As expected, Jagmohan ji called up Anil's office to check on his whereabouts, as only the front desk was on duty at that time.He was told by them that Anil had already left for home. All the loose ends of the story were scattered in front of Jagmohan ji and he was forced to believe what Anil had wanted him to believe. There was another twist in the story.

Poor Jagmohan ji was in full mood, as always, to spend his time with some soothing old melodies. He picked up some sad songs that evening and started playing, "*Dost dost na raha, pyar pyar na raha.*"

The very next morning, he felt like having an open-hearted conversation with Kavita. Kavita herself was a part of the drama being played out. She was totally indifferent and resisted talking on the topic. It was strange for Jagmohan ji when she refrained to comment on Anil's late arrivals. He tried to wheedle her to say what was on her mind, but she played her part really well.

"Papa, I can't stop him from doing what he wants and it doesn't bother my life anymore."

That remark wrenched his heart, but he tried to regain his balance. He was, however, able to gain insight into his new angle to Kavita's affair. Kavita got busy with her household chores and Jagmohan ji went to his room. He expressed his concern to Krishna ji.

"What?" It was too much for her to grasp. Krishna ji patiently listened to the whole story. She then correlated it with Kavita's sullen expression from when the couple had came back home on Friday night. It had been because of the argument they had had, but she mistook it as something else. They had nothing more to think about, as the issue was pretty clear in front of their eyes now. The main question in their minds was, "Why did it happen after all these years?"

The children had gone to school. The four of them sat down for breakfast together. A sulk sunk in at the table. There were all grownups sitting together. At a younger age, children can be guided, but what does one say to fully responsible adults? Krishna ji gave a sniff, expressing her resentment with regard to the changes happening in the family. Jagmohan ji looked at her, while Anil and Kavita pretended to ignore her. At last, Krishna ji broke the silence. She started asking questions related to Anil's work at office. Jagmohan ji also started beating around the bush, giving sermons on healthy relationships. All of a sudden, Anil spoke, "Papa, why do you spend all of your time with these old songs or with your other old friends and not with Ma? And Mamma, why do you go to your *mahila samaaj* meetings and remain so stiff at home. It is simple; we tend to like spending time with like-minded people, and there is nothing wrong with that."

Anil's words left a ruffling impact on their minds. He knew that it was not the most correct way to make them realize the importance of love. It indubitably became a matter of deep concern for the parents, because children at any age need the guiding support of their parents. But the problem here was that the children were adamant on fulfilling their own wishes, over the health of their relationship and had all erroneous notions about it.

Anil just wanted his parents to comprehend their problems of middle age and understand that they really needed some backend support. After all, the parents would have experienced those very problems in their own time and Anil expected them to be more accommodating than just demanding. He felt a dire need to express his feelings to his parents, that expectations cannot be single sided and that they too expected a certain degree of understanding and help from their parents. In the present cosmopolitan milieu, when even the most basic food is adulterated and we live a sedentary lifestyle, middle age is reduced to living like remote operated machines. Too much is expected from them in the name of duty and responsibility. This tangle angle of their life becomes a double edged sword. Neither can they accept the redundant demands of their teenage children, nor can they deal with the strong headedness of their old parents. It was high time for people related to them to understand their own responsibility too. That was surely the high way to make them realize this, but then sometimes, "All is fair in love."

Krishna ji could not blame her daughter-in-law for her imprudent behavior, as all her focus had now shifted to the impudence of her own son. She found herself truly helpless. It was not difficult for anyone to correlate Kavita's sedition with Anil's audacity to go against her. For Krishna ji, Kavita had always been an ideal person as far as relationships were concerned, so it did not seem fair on her son's part to oppress her like that. The major dilemma for her at that time was that she could not vindicate Kavita for having inviting someone else into her life.

"The problem is not as meagre as we thought," she told Jagmohan ji. "We have been too busy in ourselves that we failed to notice the corrosiveness that developed in their relationship." She was really worried about the mess that had been created in their lives.

A serious introspection was underway. Any age comes with its own complications. With growing age, it becomes all the more important to realize and accept things gracefully. Acceptance is the bottom line of all relationships. Accepting and realizing one's mistakes is the true sign of graceful ageing. It was time for self analysis and Krishna ji sat patiently to observe the intricate details of her son's relationship, so that some corrective action could be taken. She took this testing episode as a learning experience and didn't let her ego come in the way of her problem solving. Jagmohan ji was also of the same frame of mind. Both of them analysed the situation and talked about Anil's thought provoking questions too. They were also aware that the love had faded away from their lives a long time ago and that they had got habitual of each other. It was time for them to rethink and re-establish their bond too. It was not so difficult to work out. It was indispensable to break that rebellious streak in their children, that too at an age when they were expected to adhere to the norms of the society.

Kavita was not too pleased about dragging them into this puzzled situation. She really wished to clarify all doubts and misunderstandings to relieve her in laws of the trauma they were facing. But then, she stopped herself from doing so.

Chapter 22

A New Character

A drastic change came about in the approach of the family members towards the situation at home. The long awaited coordination between the different age groups at home was finally happening. Everyone had realized the need for maintaining an organized system of working. Chaotic mornings got replaced by peaceful ones. The children did not make much fuss anymore and the parents withheld their unnecessary expectations. Perhaps that was the after effect of the revolt that had turned the relationships which they had long taken for granted. Krishna ji tried her level best to bring back her son's lost concern for her daughter-in-law. At the same time, both of them efficiently played their part by maintaining their distance and talking only when required in front of everyone at home.

"Anil, let's go out for a family vacation. It's been a long time since you planned anything like that. It will be a good change," Krishna ji tried to coax him in the hope of bringing back the old times.

Without paying any heed to his mother, Anil carelessly declared, "I want to invite my colleague home for dinner tonight. She wants to meet everyone."

Krishna ji flinched at Anil's troubling behavior.

An ominous silence prevailed in the house.

Anil looked at his mother, as if expecting a positive reply from her for his strange demand.

His mother, who was brilliant at handling all kinds of problems, found herself at a lack of wits to respond to such a situation, which was beyond her scope of understanding.

It was difficult for Anil too to show that reticence on his face, but that was the demand of his character. He had never played hide and seek with his mother in such a way before, but he played the game so seriously this time, without letting the varied emotions of his mother deter his intentions. After all, he was convinced why he needed to do it.

Leaving his mother to her thoughts in silence, he left for work.

After a while, Kavita came and told Krishna ji that she was going out to meet Aparna.

It was really disheartening for her to handle all this. She patiently waited for Tanay to come back from school. It was high time to let the children know about the troubles in their parents' life. She knew that technology would be of great help in sorting things out again, and a good coordination with the new generation would certainly help to mend the lost relationship. A team effort was required to work upon the serious mission of reuniting the family.

That reunion was still a faraway elusive dream, but the crisis at home became conducive in bringing the two different worlds together. Everyone had to bear the cost. The world of the teenagers amalgamated with the world of the oldies, in hope to restore the peace of their loved ones' lives. The irony of the situation was that they were working together to bring harmony to that very middle segment of the house, which went into discord trying to integrate them in the first place. Finally, Krishna ji disclosed her penny-full of thoughts to Tanay and asked him to try everything he could to find out about 'NEEL'.

Anil and Kavita on the other hand planned a secret meeting to discuss the game plan further. Kavita was really curious to know what Anil had planned ahead. Eagerly, she asked Anil about it.

"Patience, madam. Let the fruit grow ripe before you pluck it," Anil remarked with a smile.

"Anil, tell me, yaar. It's churning my stomach now." She had started to lose her nerves by then.

"Hello, Kavita ji. How are you? I have heard a lot about you, but I see now that it was barely enough," a stranger walked upto them an dragged a chair to come sit next to them.

Kavita gave him an confused look, as if asking him, "Who are you?"

That stranger and Anil shared an affirmative glance with each other and then Anil turned to Kavita and said, "This is Subraneel, a Mumbai based businessman who has won many accolades for his work. He is the answer to all your doubts."

Kavita looked at him again. The guy, who seemed to be in his late thirties, looked quite decent, sober and erudite. She still had a dazed expression on her face.

"Dear," Anil started, "You asked me why I was pulling Rakshanda into our story. It's because of Subraneel. He is the new character in our story, your NEEL."

Kavita felt a little embarrassed at the last phrase,'your Neel'. She still felt too muddle headed to react to this new twist in the tale.

"There is no need of hauling anyone into our life." She seemed unhappy. And then, looking at Subraneel, she said, "Sorry, no offence to you."

"I knew you will overreact. Please give me a chance to explain, at least," Anil told her.

"Fine," she sat back, testing her patience.

"It's not about us anymore. It is about him and Rakshanda," Anil gave her the gist of everything with those words.

"Kavita ji, your husband is a gem of a person. He made me realize the importance of a life partner. He gave me the last hope to win her back in my life, but it'll be impossible without your help. I want to live for her till my last breath," Subraneel pleaded.

"Give him a chance, Kavita. I will narrate their entire story to you later, but please think about it. If our efforts are able to save a dying relationship, wouldn't that be the victory of LOVE?Don't you always say that love constitutes our very existence and that no one should be deprived of it?Please, for the sake of LOVE, approve it."

Kavita was not too hard to melt and agreed to play her part as written by Anil.

Anil further gave them both an outline of what was to be done ahead.

While he was explaining things to them, Kavita looked at this new form of him in wonder. She knew that her husband was the best, but getting a peek into this disposition of his character, made her fall for him all over again. Anil read his wife's expression and the two of them looked into each other's eyes lovingly. The way they were lost in each other, anyone could have been convinced that their relationships was beyond just the heart and soul.

Subraneel, on the other hand, had started to feel really intensely about Rakshanda.

Chapter 23

The Execution of the Plan

Anil invited Rakshanda to dinner at home. Though she was not too keen on getting involved in such a program, Anil convinced her with his words about the comfort of a family environment. He spoke with such genuine concern that Rakshanda, who always acted as a tough lady, agreed to the proposal. Somewhere deep down, she missed being in a family environment herself. It was indispensable to get the lady into the loop, in order to get her into the rhythm of developing relations again. A broken heart takes time to heal, and with her, that healing had never probably happened. She bought a nice bouquet and a cake for the family. After all, the last time she had experienced such a family environment was three years ago when her parents were still alive. She lost them in an accident and since then, she had been staying alone, hiding behind a harsh world of masks. That's what she was to the world and to the people living in it, a MASK. She had it on at all times, especially when she had to interact with people around her.

She rang the door bell, unaware of the game plan. She greeted everyone with warmth and tried to adjust to the family environment. One who has been longing for something, relishes it the best when they finally get it. Within no time, she found herself enjoying the congenial environment at home. Anil gave her special attention, which was not usual for Rakshanda, but she ignored it thinking that perhaps he was only trying to make her feel more comfortable as a guest. However, she did notice a distance between Anil and Kavita.

Krishna ji liked her personality and had it been a normal situation, she would have reciprocated to the lady with the same warmth, but at that time, she had planned to show the lady something else entirely. It was Tanay's idea to make this lady jealous of their family. The silent eye coordination between the four was at its functional best that night. Tanvi quickly fetched her parents' wedding album to show to the lady how much her parents loved each other. Rakshanda indulged herself in the family environment and gelled quite well with everyone. Anil did not feel the need to forcefully direct the drama, as it was playing out exactly as he had wanted it to in its natural form. While bidding them goodbye, Rakshanda told Kavita how lucky she was for having such a wonderful family. "I envy you," she said with all her emotions, hitting the nail right on its head. Anil realised that his purpose had been achieved and that he had successfully killed two birds with one stone. On one side, he had made Rakshanda realize the importance of love, while on the other, he had proved to his family his inclination towards her.

After seeing her off, Kavita and Anil went into their room, while the teens and the grandparents sat together for another secret conference to decide on their strategy further. Dadu dawdled around the room. Everyone was going through conflicting emotions. They imagined her taking the place of Kavita, and shivers ran down their spines, expressing their disapproval.

"No way, dadi, she can't replace mamma," Tanvi said, feeling upset.

"Even I can't imagine her in place of Kavita," Krishna ji said in a depressed manner.

"I think Anil has lost it," Jagmohan ji fumed.

Though Tanay felt distraught, he couldn't stop thinking about how to solve this problem.

"I have an idea, Dadi.We need to show her the strength of our love. What say, we call her for Saumya *di*'s wedding? We will prove to her how much dad really loves mom." Although Tanay spoke with conviction, he himself was in grave doubt about his statement.

Krishna ji's eyes sparkled up at the idea.

"You are right, Tanay. I must say, you are really intelligent. You remember how your dad and mom sang and danced at her engagement function. I am sure those memories will bring them together again."

Anil, who had been listening to them from behind the wall, giggled and walked quietly back to his room.

He felt guilty for having paid so much attention to Rakshanda all evening, and now turned to look at Kavita with eyes full of emotional longing.

Making love with someone who is deeply understanding of your own self is always exciting. Who says that middle aged people get so used to it that they hardly enjoy it with the same person anymore? It's perhaps a matter of perception only. When love comes to its original form, it becomes more about giving pleasure to the partner, rather than seeking it for oneself. And when it is about giving, happiness is but natural. Kavita's eyes twinkled with affection for her husband. His hands moved over her body and he looking into her eyes as he expressed his emotions:

"Shame-e-haseen, bata teri justajoo kya hai

Jo teri aagosh mein hai, wo mera lamha hai."

(Beautiful night! What's in your heart just tell me

Each moment that lies in you, belongs to me.)

They lived and loved each moment completely. Anil stroked her hair with caressing fingers silently. Kavita broke the silence and said, "What next, dear?"

"Let the spark turn into a fire, *jaaneman,*" Anil smiled and snuggled next to her in bed. Kavita slipped into a comfortably sleep as well. It was a beautiful night after all.

The next morning, before Jagmohan ji woke up, Anil went to the drawing room and fell asleep on the recliner there. He knew that his father was an early riser, and this was the best way to show them that it had been a bad night for them. Kavita altered her facial expressions dramatically as well to show her disagreement regarding whatever had happened the previous night.

It was a Friday morning and everyone knew that Kavita would spend time out with Neel that evening. Krishna ji was eagerly waiting for Kavita to come and inform her about her plan to go out. It was finally time to introduce Subraneel to everyone. Kavita left her phone at the dining table on purpose. As a message pinged on it, their provocation to pick it up came naturally.

A messaged flashed from Neel, which read:

"*At Chuski, 5 P.M. You di...*"

Krishna ji read the message. What she had wanted to know was clear enough and the rest was presumed. "He must be asking why she didn't turn up to meet him last Friday.He has changed the venue too this time.Very smart, but he doesn't know the consequences of messing with us," she murmured.

Kavita declared her plan to go out to her. Krishna ji waited for Tanay to come back and plan the next move. The whole house was rapt with an anxious excitement for that evening.

Chapter 24

Look, Who is Peeping In?

Kavita found it very difficult. Not only did she have to meet someone else, but also had to pretend to be in love with that person. It was too difficult for her to conform to the situation. Moreover, she was nervous because her family had been chasing her and she knew about it. She never wanted to do something with such a pinch of salt in it, but that situation was out of her control.

A ping on her phone made her realize that she was getting late. Her phone had a message from Anil. Her vibe had already conveyed her dubious state of mind to him. The message was:

"(Read and delete)

Dear Kavita, I love you and I strongly believe in your courage. You are my only reason to smile. It is difficult for me to see you with someone else too, but I know you will never let LOVE bow down to someone's ego. And don't worry, I will be there too. Cheer up and think as if you are coming to meet me."

Kavita's eyes lit up on reading that loving note. She deleted the message and got ready for the meeting.

As soon as she left, it was time for the detective team to tighten up their belts too. As they got into a taxi, Krishna ji instructed her husband, "You and Tanvi go to the music café near the meeting point and keep your eyes and ears open. Make sure that no one recognizes you there."

"Dadi, what was the need of this moustache on my face. It feels horrible," Tanay said, feeling uncomfortable in his detective getup.

"And I feel like a small kid in this frock," Tanvi complained.

"It is so that nobody recognizes us," Jagmohan ji replied confidently. "Just look at your dadi. She looks like a perfect detective in those jeans and sunglasses," he smiled.

"And you need a carrot, my Karamchand *jasoos*,"Krishna ji said in style.

Now that's what a family means. Even in tense situations, a family finds ways to be lively.

The taxi ride ended in a jiffy.

The evening had many events wrapped into its folds. Subraneel and Kavita sat talking over a cup of coffee. Krishna ji tried to peep in with caution. Kavita was feeling uneasy due to the dramatic nature of the whole situation. Subraneel tried his best to make it more comfortable for her.

"It is not easy for me either, Kavita ji." he said, "We are all actors here. Our destiny has designed this platform for us and when destiny directs, it has to be for something good."

Kavita closed her eyes for a few seconds to gather her courage to get into her acting avatar. She opened her eyes and felt ready to be in style. She smiled and blushed, pretending to enjoying his company.

The spy team kept an undeterred watch on them, unprepared for the other jerk that was coming their way. Anil entered the café with Rakshanda just then. They took a table near Kavita's and took their seats in such a way that Rakshanda could see them. Anil placed an order for two cups of tea. They had gone for some meeting together and on their way back, Anil had strongly insisted for her to have a cup of tea with him. Kavita and Subraneel suddenly laughed out loud on purpose, but in a carefree manner. Anil and Rakshanda instinctively turned towards them. Rakshanda was baffled at the sight. Meanwhile, Krishna ji, along with Tanay, made their way towards the exit. She did not want to be involved in a fuss in public. It took a while for Rakshanda to regain her composure. She quickly turned to Anil and asked, "Isn't that your wife?"

With a blank expression on his face, he nodded his head in affirmation. She grew quiet upset and expressed her wish to leave. Anil paid the bill and they moved out of the café.

So far, things were going exactly as per Anil's plan.Everyone from home had had a glimpse of that jarring situation. Back home, Kavita pretended as if nothing had happened, precisely according to Anil's script. Dinner was laid, but everyone was in a sour mood. Finally, Anil broke the silence and set the issue ablaze. "Who was that man with you at the café?" Any rational man would have asked such a question after seeing his wife with someone else. Kavita had not expected such rudeness from him. She fumbled, "C…can we go inside our room and talk?"

"Don't change the topic," he grumbled.

"Okay, it had all been happening under the covers till now, but if you wish to unveil it tonight, then so be it. Did I ask you, why you invited that lady to our house last night?"

In his heart of hearts, Anil praised his wife for her excellent acting skills.

This was not the kind of behavior expected from them. Parents, as well as children, watched them in shock. The stage characters had swapped their roles. Usually the fight used to be between the teens and the oldies, with the middle generation acting as spectators, but the roles had reversed now. After a while, Jagmohan ji interrupted them with a gruff voice.

"Can both of you behave like normal people? I had never expected such a situation in our house. Your children are still growing up and you have responsibilities on your head. You should be paying more attention to your children rather than thinking about yourselves."

" Why, papa? Why is the baggage of all this responsibility only on us? Why should it only be us to bear the heat from both sides? For the sake of these responsibilities and ethics, I won't let the few remaining golden years of my life go to waste. I had gone on pleading with everyone at home to maintain peace here, but I was being blamed for everything regardless. No one spoke for me then," Kavita complained.She stopped to look at Anil and then continued, "I left my career for this house. Even you have no time to spare for me or your family. If all ethical norms apply on me, then what about you? Everyone is only concerned about himself in this madhouse. Why do you expect from me then? The person I met today, he cares for me. He does not demand anything in return. He is a good friend and I don't think that married people can't befriend people of the opposite sex. I have no complains if Anil likes to spend some quality time with his colleague. Then why I am answerable to anyone for doing the same?" She was filled with acrimony.

"Don't you dare blame me for anything," Anil said, getting defensive. "I have always taken care of the finances of this house, while you have never had any time for me. You are always busy with something or the other. And Mamma," he turned to his mother, "You have always been so proud of your CRP(Child Rearing Practices). Are these two not your children? Why are only parents responsible for everything, can't the grandparents share that responsibility? And these never ending teenage tantrums, I felt fed up of even coming back to this house everyday. In so many years, there hardly have been any moments of solace for me. I regret getting married at all." Anil had let out all his grief regarding his circumstances in one go.

It was of no use trying to mediate between them at that time. Everyone felt shaken due to that unexpected war of words between Anil and Kavita.

Chapter 25

The Flashback

Kavita and Anil entered their room sullenly. They felt bad for the kind of torture they were making their family undergo, but no gain ever came out of no pain. Anil looked at Kavita and told her, "Just a few days more, dear. Good things come to those who wait."

Kavita tried to bring herself out of that sullen mood and asked Anil about Subraneel and Rakshanda."How did you rope them into our story?" she asked.

"Destiny, dear. You remember the day when you got caught and we thought that everyone will get to know about us?"

"Yeah! I felt so humiliated. How can I forget that?"

"The very next day at office, I was thinking of ways to tackle it. See! Had they known that we are having the secret affair, there would be no crisis situation at all and we would have had to face their punitive actions. So, I wanted something to prove their story right, in order to make them learn some coordination. God actually sent Subraneel right then to our rescue. That day, Rakshanda hadn't turned up for work and Subraneel came to enquire about Rakshanda." Anil went on to narrate the entire scene to Kavita.

"Hi! I am Subraneel."

"Hello, sir. I am Anil." He shook hands with him and offered him a seat.

"Can you give me the address of Ms. Rakshanda. I want to meet her," he said, coming straight to the point.

"Sorry, sir. But I cannot give you her contact details."

"Mr. Anil, are you married?"

Anil looked at him in a confused expression.

"I am sorry, what?" he asked politely, as his profession did not allow him to be rude. "Why do you want her address?"

Subraneel heaved a deep sigh. Then, he started narrating his story.

"Those were the young years of our life. Rakshanda and I were all youthful and zealous about life. We were studying at the same college, pursuing our M.B.A. degrees from Pune. She was just as inspirational as she is today. Eloquent and vibrant, she always wanted to create a niche for herself in the P.R. sector. I had a huge family business and I aspired to expand it further. We were so in love with each other. When my mother lost her long standing battle with cancer, I found myself dismayed. She then encouraged me to open a cancer hospital and even handled all paper work to start it off. I am her biggest fan. I remember, all our fellow friends always swore by our love. Then at the campus interviews, she got selected by a training organization. It had always been her dream job, mentoring people around her. She possesses the beautiful art of impressing people with the magic spell of her charm, and you already know how well she can play with words. It makes you want to prostrate in front of her. We fell apart due to her corporate indulgences and my business. We barely got the time to spend with each other." Subraneel was lost in his reminiscences and Anil was completely engrossed in it too.

They glanced at each other and Anil could see the pain in his eyes.

"Then, what happened?" Anil asked with curiosity.

"The most exciting day of my life arrived. I booked a private yacht to propose to her. It was so fulfilling to see her so full of life. When I proposed to her, she made me feel like the luckiest man alive by saying 'YES'. That day felt like living through a complete era in itself. We postponed all our commitments to take the vows for a lifetime's commitment. Those beautiful moments are still so fresh in my mind even after 8 long years and I shall cherish them forever." He had described his 'love' in such a beautiful fashion that Anil could not help but imagine his own bond with Kavita.

'Love, whether in love marriages or arrange marriages, has the same effect, I guess,' Anil thought, while Subraneel re-lived through his moments.

With a long sigh, he continued, "That happiness was only short lived, however. It was my fault. I could have stopped her when she told me 'Let me go'. Her words still haunt me today when I have everything, but no one to enjoy it with. We live in a man's world where we are expected to earn and they are supposed to take care of our homes. Her job demanded too much travel and I expected her to give up her job and join me in my business. She tried to convince me a lot, but I was perhaps stuck in the ego of my superiority. Honestly, being a man actually cost me my life. After she left, I got so busy in my work that there was no time left for anything else in my life. Last month, I saw her in Mumbai during a conference and she had the same depth in her eyes as before. I tried to approach her, but she bluntly refused. I somehow managed to reach her and proposed to her again, but she told me that she has already deleted my chapter from her life. I don't know what to do now. Since then, I have been trying to find her and when I finally got her office address, I came here." With a stutter in his voice, he asked, "Is she still single?"

Anil could understand Rakshanda's stern attitude now by correlating it with her harsh past. He answered, "Yes! She is still single, and she never allows anyone to come too close to her."

"I know it is my attitude that turned her into stone and I so wish I could soften her. I will stay here till I wash away all the bad memories in her mind about me," Subraneel said in a morose manner. "So that's about me. Tell me something about your life," he asked Anil.

Anil felt himself out of the stranger bias against Subraneel and found himself wanting to share his story with him. He opened up to him and told him everything about his secret yet open affair.

Subraneel found that quite amazing. He was ready to accept anything for Rakshanda, but knew that it would be difficult to take her out of her bitter memories.

Anil told him that it would not be wise to meet the grief stricken lady all of a sudden. Thinking about a solution, Anil came up with the idea of linking both the stories together. He shared his piece of mind with Subraneel. He wanted Rakshanda back at any cost and he knew that it was not going to be easy. It was imperative for them to ignite those lost feelings of love in her. It was just like filling old wounds with the new, for her stiffness was beyond control otherwise.

Anil had been searching for a solution for his own problem and destiny planned to answer it on its own. It had been Anil's dream to direct a film once and now he got to pen down the real drama of his life. He laughed at the situations and told himself, "Sometimes, it is not necessity which is the mother of invention, but simply monotony is."

He planned and wrote a complete script of how things would move over the coming days.

Subraneel then planned an event which was to be organized by Anil's hotel. Anil purposely took Rakshanda there with him, which in turn was mistaken as something else by Jagmohan ji. At the event, when Rakshanda met Subraneel, the hidden friction between them was easily palpable. As a business client, Anil treated Subraneel with complete professional ethics. He even offered him stay at their hotel, which Rakshanda resisted, but it was purposely done. Being in the hospitality industry, she knew how to cover up her discomforts.

The next move was to call Rakshanda over for dinner and give her the feel of a family. At the same time, he had to prove himself unethical in front of his family.

Coming back to the present moment, Anil told Kavita "The rest, you already know."

She smiled and felt grateful for her life. After all, it was unfolding in such a way that each leaf felt like a new one every time. She slept with a feeling of gratitude.

Chapter 26

Muddle of the Puzzle

It was undoubtedly a stressful night for the teens and the grandparents in the house. Tanay and Tanvi had always looked at their parents as an ideal couple. For the first time now, they realized that there were many troubles in their married life. It was a matter of deep concern for the elders of the house that the teens were having to go through that emotional turmoil at such a tender age. It was not easy for both of them to bear the shock, but the grandparents tried their best to calm them down.

The experienced Krishna ji gently stroked Tanay's back to give him some solace. With a deep sense of understanding, she brought the children out of their blurred imaginations. Very wisely, she made them understand the rough patch which emerges sometimes in one's life when all the relations get busy in themselves, creating a vacuum in a person's life. She gave them the insight to introspect on their own behavior of having taken their parents for granted.

Tanay felt a special admiration for his dadi. He, along with Tanvi, hugged her tightly. She kissed them and told them to release the pressure on themselves and that all will be fine soon.

After comforting the children, Krishna ji went back to her own room. She looked at Jagmohan ji, who seemed equally worried. It is not that the elders don't want to take responsibility. It just happens that at some point of time, growing age starts to show its signs in the middle aged and they start feeling tired. The running around, which had been easy during the initial years of their marriage, became too difficult with the passage of time. It becomes tiring for the middle aged to take care of all the responsibilities and at that time, even their togetherness becomes a routine. When you are part of a routine, life becomes like a machine. There arises the need for a balancing factor then which can guide the children to think about their parent's needs too. The elders at that point of time should take the responsibility to accept the view points of their middle aged children. If we get into a debate, then even our elders can't be blamed. The things which they had left years ago can't be expected to be shared again. Perhaps the expectations from both ends are not communicated properly and that becomes the reason behind the generation leap. Beyond that, the societal boundaries are such that we make ourselves captive inside our own shells and don't wish to release our stress.

A serious self analysis happened that night for Krishna ji, as she thought of ways to break the barrier between the different generations.

"At every age, life has its own flavour," she thought.

They struggled to sleep.

It took a while for things to normalize at home. However, it was not difficult to prove that Kavita was meeting 'that guy' for her next jewellery assignment. The baked story turned real when she actually showed her designs to Subraneel. He got really impressed with her refined taste. He offered her an assignment to create a design catalogue for his retail stores. This way, their excuses turned into reality.

Saumya's wedding was approaching and Anil wanted to serve something right in the middle so that Rakshanda and Subraneel could be invited without any trouble. The drama sequence was ready and Anil initiated the plan. He entered his mother's room with with a dense expression.

Krishna ji tried to read his intense face. She assumed that he had come to ask for her forgiveness for whatever he had been doing.

"Sorry, son, but you started it. You were rude to her and never even offered to take her out somewhere. Your illicit behavior forced her to break her own barriers too. Go and talk to her and clear your misunderstandings," Krishna ji spoke impromptu in a stern tone.

"Oh! That was just a usual business deal. She got another assignment. I have no issues regarding that. You don't worry about it. I just came here to tell you that I will not be attending Saumya's wedding. I have some events lined upon those dates." He was equally prompt, but casual. He didn't wait for her to even react, but just walked out.

This caught them unprepared. It actually hit her hard because till then, she had not assessed the extent of the seriousness of the matter. She had assumed till then that it was nothing more than a casual inclination towards another person due to the monotony of the middle age, but things now seemed to be getting worse with each passing day and she could not do anything to control the circumstances.

Jagmohan ji was a wonderful support to her at that time. She recovered from that shock with immense difficulty. She had never expected such thoughtless attitude from her children. Her standards about marriage were undergoing scrutiny themselves, and she felt very disturbed due to that.

A marriage is not about testing the limits or setting benchmarks or even defining targets. It is a relationship that is graced with complete involvement towards every one involved in it. Surrender, not sacrifice; adaptation, not tolerance; fun, not mundane; enjoyment, not service; love, not duty. But how many in this world enjoy marriages in this form? It has become a give and take relationship in this world. But it is such a beautiful relationship where one complements the other in such a way that both blend into one identity. It's a relationship where one feels incomplete without the other. This uniqueness defines their romance. It is not just the physical bond, but a feeling that transcends deep into the heart and soul. Sounds unrealistic? But it does happen. Very few are able to enjoy their bond in this form, while the rest are just married. Krishna ji had always measured a relationship against such ideals and had always given full marks to her children for having maintained such standards. However, what was happening in front of her eyes now was definitely the obverse.

She was aware that a huge gap had developed between Jagmohan ji and herself and that they were just living in a marriage of name. She was like a rock and her husband never questioned her. At times, his inert attitude was reflected in their children too, but he always believed that his wife had it all. This crisis situation, however, filled up that gap between them and she cried her heart out on his shoulder.

"I involved myself with all my social activities after you and the kids left me alone at home. They got busy in their studies and you, in making money. I buried all my wishes for the sake of a better future for the kids and kept standing as a pillar of strength for everyone. I don't know where I missed out."

Jagmohan ji supported her as best as he could. He knew that whatever she had said was right.

May be it is the same story for all married couples.They get so busy dealing with all the responsibilities that they don't find the time to even sit with each other. The surprising part of this story is that the partners in sex can't show even the slightest of intimacy in front of their children. This is still such a taboo in the society for the middle age to touch or kiss in front of their children. In fact, they feel guilty if they are caught doing so. This kind of distance maintained during the day time depletes their physical quotient over the course of time. Their steaming and storming long hours of sex sessions get converted into a two minute noodles exercise; just another routine job. That carefree physical touch goes out of their lives due to the presence of their children and parents.

Krishna ji realized for the first time that it was time to break such barriers and understand love in its actual form. There had to be a start somewhere, sometime.

Chapter 27

Traces of Love

It is really ironical that children who go through puberty are taught about sex, but not about taking care of relationships. They are not taught that they'll need to give some space to their parents too. They know that they themselves are the proof of a sexual relationship between their parents, but if their parents show any kind of physical intimacy in front of them, they feel awkward. Privacy is everyone's birthright, but couple space is also the need of the hour. Showing love in front of your children and parents is still considered indecent in our societal rule book. This is the tradition that is being followed by generations after generations and the slack goes on.

Krishna ji somewhat understood the problem and could connect her own past experiences with Kavita's situation. She had seen traces of love still left between them and believed that their bond could be regenerated. She looked at it as just a distortion, brought about due to a lack of time for each other and nothing more. It was that stage where she could finally reach the root cause of the problem. She also understood that it was time to make the younger generation realize the importance of relationships in one's life. It was indispensable for parents to inculcate that instinctual value of 'respecting one's partner/spouse' in their children. If we teach them this value, then they would also learn to nurture their relationships, and the best way to teach anything is to do it yourself. Children always find it easier to follow when they observe a certain behavior in front of their eyes. It is our duty to educate our children to honour their parents' couple space. Their parents cannot be just their caregivers. They were husband and wife, even before they became parents.

An increased rate of divorces, extramarital affairs and solitude perhaps are the consequences of a lack of sensitivity towards relationships. This middle age depression is quite common these days. The woman loses her maiden name, to bear the name of her husband. She wishes to seek out her own identity, but becomes used to her family needs. The father, on the other side, finds himself overburdened by the family demands. All through this while, the couple space gets lost. The persons whom they saw in each other and fell in love with, cease to exist at all. The careless girl shapes up into a responsible woman and the carefree brat assumes charge of so many lives. Time flies and life starts to run after demands. The couple space is lost due to multiple responsibilities. Another bizarre part is that when the couple wants to enjoy freely, time constraints hold them back and when only time is left, health constraints come into place.

Krishna ji could relate to this whole irony of time in relationships and the need to accept that couple space. She realized it was high time to talk openly about their problems and relationship needs. That Friday evening when Kavita and Anil were not at home, she gave a beautiful message on love and relationships to her grandchildren. She chose to talk seriously on this seemingly trivial topic. Dadu was sitting with her too when she tried to break the communication barrier on love and relationships.

"Dear children," she started, "You must have studied about puberty in your biology class by now. Your body undergoes many hormonal changes during this time. I am sure that you must be noticing such changes, and getting under stress is quite natural in this process. Feeling attracted towards the opposite sex is again a part of these changes. Our body prepares us to reproduce more of our kind. You must have learnt about reproduction in human beings. Bearing children is one of the biggest responsibilities for us and every person should evaluate himself or herself before taking this responsibility. It is fair enough that children must be guided and guarded by their parents till the time they become capable of making their own choices but the children must be made aware of the consequences borne by their decisions too. You need to be cautious enough before getting into a relationship and try to understand the implications of such a choice. As time passes, children grow up to become adults. At an appropriate age after comprehending the importance of relationships, they should take up this responsibility. Getting into a relationship calls for a beautiful amalgamation between two different individuals, with different backgrounds. It means respecting each other's individuality and adapting accordingly. They make love, indulge in physical and emotional intimacy and vow to start a family. They bear children, take their responsibility, maintain a lifestyle and work together for a better future. In this process of running around, the two individuals try to complete each other. Kids, I want you to understand this phrase 'in this process'. *Beta,* at times due to increasing responsibilities, they start losing out on their intimacy and find themselves standing apart. Time flies and they become a part of a routine. At that point, they become emotionally week and start looking for others outside of their relationship. The system may call it illegal, but each individual has his or her own reasons and we should not question their viewpoint. Instead, we should try to understand their justifications and find out the reason behind this rift in their compatibility."

Krishna ji looked at her audience with great affinity.

She continued, "I have realized that due to all of us, your parents have not been able to express their love to each other too often and now find themselves seeking that attention. After all, all of us human beings have that natural urge to be loved. It is time for us to realize that we have not put in any effort in making your parents love their relationship. It is because of us that they could not relish their togetherness. I am sure, however, that traces of love are still present in their hearts and we can get them together again. Let's return to them their due."

Tanay and Tanvi found her words really relevant. They understood the need to give their parents that quality time with one another, which had badly been required. The discontent in their parents' marriage had come about only because they had failed to realize the importance of couple space. That self assessment was badly needed and it helped them cope with all kinds of emotional turmoil. They understood in an instant what their dadi was talking about. They vowed together to bring back the joys of love in their parents' life.

Jagmohan ji got very emotional at the sight of that union. He looked at his wife with mixed feelings of love and pride. He had always trusted the fine wisdom of his wife, but at that point of time, he expressed this appreciation and admiration to the lady of his life. Expressing his intense emotions, he confessed in front of the young ones, "I love you, Krishna. It's been ages that we have shared this friendship with each other. I promise you that I won't spend most of my time with those oldies, talking about politics and religion anymore. Let's celebrate our togetherness and love this bond till our last breath." He hugged her and she kissed him on his cheek.

Blushing red, they broke the so called traditional slack.

"Clap!Clap!Clap! A huge round of applause for our super cool dadu and dadi. You taught us what we would never have learned about love. Dadu! Don't you have an appropriate song on this?" Tanay exclaimed.

"*Khullam khulla pyar karenge hum dono.*"

Everyone burst into laughter.

Tanvi switched on the recording from Saumya's engagement. The spy dadi continued to think about the problem while looking for an answer in that Punjabi song. She tried to look at all possible outcomes of the events that had taken place in last couple of months. She could co-relate many things, like Anil purposely talking about Rakshanda and making Kavita jealous about it. Probably, she had also found someone to lean on. Soon, she made all the permutations and combinations in her mind and prepared for her game. She told the kids to just pay attention to their studies and not to take much stress about the problems at home.

She instructed Tanvi to solve her maths doubts with dadu and then asked Tanay to help her out with operating the internet. She wanted some contact numbers. All through, one thing was very clear, "Perfection lies in overlooking imperfections."

Chapter 28

The Masterstroke

The family was undergoing a crisis situation without knowing that all of it had been fabricated by Anil. Everything was unconventionally planned in such a fashion that they had naturally imbibed into the desired characters without realizing the dramatic nature of it. However, he had never expected such stupendous results to come out of their drama. He thanked his destiny for having shown him the perfect family bond. Now it was time to play the other part of story which extended to Rakshanda.

It was natural for Rakshanda to feel bad every time she saw Subraneel with Kavita at the hotel. Kavita would often come to the hotel with her files for the sake of her so called work related meetings. After all, Subraneel was a guest at their hotel. The apparent growing compatibility between them was enough to break down the strong lady. Sitting in her cabin, she fiddled with the paper weight and evaluated her life in terms of relationships. That vacuum disturbed her outward stiffness. She had contracted the periphery of her life to the extent that she had no one to look upon on returning home each day.

"Why do people in this world still look at a single working lady and consider her to be always available? Why do they assume her to be absconding from getting married? Why is the choice of a woman not valued? Why are things always forced upon her? Why she always need a validation?" Her mind was full of hatred towards the gender bias in the society. Ridiculing all biases that a woman has to face, she had accepted her dignity to overshadow all her problems. But then, all those wounds that she had tried hard to fill over a period of time were being scratched by Subraneel again.

"No," she told herself. "I was never the Aunt Sally of your game and will never allow you to make me feel like that, Subraneel." She stopped fiddling with the paper weight and spun it on its axis for a couple of seconds. She kept staring at it till it stopped and then dialed Anil's number.

"Anil, can you please come to my office?" she asked.

Anil was pretending to be the victim of whole drama that was going on between Kavita and Subraneel. He was actually waiting for Rakshanda's burning jealousy to reach its peak. When he got that call, he could not stop smiling. It was that awaited fateful day, perhaps. He knocked at the door of her cabin.

"Come in, please," she said politely.

"Hello, Rakshanda," Anil replied in a courteous manner.

"Are you comfortable with your wife coming here off and on to meet that guest at our hotel?" she asked him straightaway, while trying to conceal her emotions at the same time.

With a slight chuckle at the phrase 'that guest', he countered her, saying, "She is just doing her job. It's about her choices. How can I interfere with that?" Anil had actually swept a masterstroke.

She was forced to compare Anil with Subraneel. 'Anil honours his wife's wishes so much, despite them being unacceptable. If only Subraneel had respected my choices so…' she thought, feeling distraught again.

Anil purposely gave her some time to feel depressed.

"Rakshanda," he called, pulling her back to the present."All well?" He coaxed her.

"I think your wife might be having an affair with him. Please don't get me wrong, but you should tell her that it's wrong." She found herself speaking out of her usual nature.

"If she likes him, how can I stop her?" He expressed his helplessness in front of her. "And why would she listen to me. We are not on good terms anyway." He spoke slowly and with a depressed voice, expressing himself as the sufferer.

"Oh!" her voice shivered.

"What happened, Rakshanda? I have never seen you in such a state," Anil asked deliberately.

"Subraneel is my ex fiancé, you see. He is just using your wife to make me jealous. I wish we could have sorted out our differences." It was the first time ever that she had told someone about her personal life.

Things were going on as expected.

"What?" He expressed his shock.

"Surprised? It's a long story. To cut it short, I have called you here for a favour," Rakshanda said in a desperate tone.

"It will be my pleasure if I can be of any help to you, dear." Anil had consciously addressed her as 'dear'.

She was not in the frame of mind where she could assert her firmness as usual, so she fumbled, "I want to show him that I am happy without him, and that I am not affected in the least by his absurd ways. Can…can…you pretend to be in relationship with me?"

'Yes! We've hit the nail right on its head again,'he murmured under his breath.

"I'll understand if you are too uncomfortable with the idea. I will look for some other alternative." She was not feeling in her own skin at the time.

"I'm fine with it, Rakshanda. Anything for you.Moreover, I too need someone to trust," he spoke extempore.

"Can we go to the restaurant where they are sitting and have a cup of coffee together?" she asked reluctantly.

"Why not, Rakshanda?" While saying this, he quickly sent a message to Kavita, *She is coming with me to the restaurant.*

While walking towards the restaurant, Rakshanda tried to

increase her proximity with him. They reached the restaurant and she scanned the room till she saw them sitting together, looking at each other passionately. She expressed her wish to sit at the same table.

Anil went to the table and interrupted their eye contact.

"Hi! May we join you here?"

Kavita looked embarrassed, but Subraneel was as casual as before.

"Hi Anil. Hi, Rakshanda." Subraneel fulfilled the protocol. "Yeah! Sure. Please join us."

As they sat there, Subraneel and Anil glanced at each other. Subraneel then gazed at Kavita and said, "Anil, I must say, you are so lucky to have such a wonderful person in your life. She is the perfect blend of beauty and brains, and believes in traditional values too. She is extremely talented and has a deep understanding for others' tastes, sentiments and emotions." He kept singing her praises till Rakshanda's jealousy reached to the point when she got up and rushes away in tears.

"Sorry, Anil, was that too much?" Subraneel asked him.

"Not at all. We are on the right track. We just need to reach the stage where Rakshanda accepts on her own that she is still in love with you. Being jealous is very much a part of love. isn't it?" He turned to look at Kavita in a possessive way. "Who won't feel jealous if your partner praises someone else in front of you?"

"I'm sorry. I embarrassed you too. But Kavita ji, honestly, whatever I said about you is cent percent correct." Subraneel understood Anil's latent meaning and his possessiveness.

Anil answered romantically:

"T*od diye hain kehne,sunne ke usool humne*

Tera haq sirf mujhe hai, ye ehsaas kafi hai."

(It is immaterial to think what to say or to hear. I own you, this feeling is enough for me.)

He looked at them and said, "Let me handle your Rakshanda. She is broken right now."

Kavita looked at him with same possessiveness too. 'Every time, I fall for him a little more,'she thought.

Chapter 29

A Date With Another Woman

Anil knew that he had added a pinch of salt to his family's life by declaring that he would not be attending Saumya's wedding. He wanted to add even more flavour to it by giving them his valid reasons behind such a decision. Along with that, he also wanted Rakshanda to feel broken so that he could take upon the lady when she was feeling down.

It was a planned dinner date with Rakshanda. The lady had been in a bitter mood when Anil had asked her for dining out with him. She had always abstained from getting involved with anyone and for the longest time, she had kept to her own world, refraining from mingling with anyone. She just wanted to forget everything. She agreed to dine out with Anil due to her recent heartbreak again. She was not as strong as she had assumed herself to be, and bearing the pain each time was not so easy for her.

Anil wrote out the whole drama again to hit the iron when it was still hot. He asked Kavita to keep him updated with every minute detail on the phone. Then he made a call home to inform that he was going out with a client for dinner at a restaurant. He specified the name of the restaurant on purpose. That's when the drama started at home too.

"He is lying. I'm sure he is going out with that lady again," Kavita shouted.

Krishna ji had attended the call and she felt confident that Anil wouldn't lie to her. She spoke with conviction, "Don't get hyper, Kavita. It is with some client."

Seeing her faith in Anil, Kavita strongly felt an urge to reveal the truth to her mom-in-law, but she stopped herself. She tested her acting skills again by replying, "Hyper, mamma?You are telling me to not get hyper? I am least bothered. I don't care if he goes out with her every day. Besides managing finances, what has his contribution been to this house anyway? Now I am capable enough to manage that too. I really don't need anything from him. Yesterday, I asked him to join us for Saumya's wedding so that our issues might remain under covers, but he just wants to draw all curtains aside. Fine then, it doesn't affect me anymore either."

Krishna ji felt badly devastated by her attitude, but she had nothing to say. She went back to her room.

Kavita displayed an indifferent attitude at home. Krishna ji wanted to check personally whether Anil was with Rakshanda or not because Kavita had created that doubt in her mind. It was a foolproof plan and her acting skills had reached their pinnacle, so there was no chance of a break down.

Krishna ji informed at home that they had to go out for some work in the evening. It was quite obvious what was going on in her mind.

Kavita kept Anil fully informed. He left office with Rakshanda after the office hours. He had booked a private corner at the restaurant for them. He needed some time to make her feel comfortable. It was really hard to get the desired results, without letting the characters know what was written in the script. Anil just kept his fingers crossed to keep things moving as he had planned. The act had to be well timed, so both Kavita and Anil kept texting each other the entire time.

The restaurant had the perfect ambience for a conversation. Anil ordered some snacks and drinks. Light music, dim lights and a private cabin made Rakshanda feel like getting into a relationship again. In her heart of hearts, she was slowly mollifying. It had not been easy for her to see someone else in Subraneel's life, although she had come to accept her fate. With ruptured emotions, she sat silently, while her thoughts were still stuck on Subraneel's attitude towards Kavita.

Anil broke the silence."I can't stay with her anymore. I also feel that she is in a relationship with him. I too need someone to fill up that gap in my life. She always remained busy with the kids before and never paid any attention to me. I feel like breaking all ties with her, but just because of my children, I am helpless. You know what happened last night? It's her sister's daughter's wedding next month and she hardly cares about asking me properly to come along, while she has already personally invited Subraneel even before the cards have reached us. I will not go there at any cost. When there is nothing left between us, why should I care about this social pressure anymore? Am I the only one responsible for it?"

Anil noticed a wavering expression on her face. Her ears were only receptive to the single sentence that Kavita had invited Subraneel for the wedding, the rest was detail. Anil knew that he had done his job and had left another string open in her mind.

A message pinged on his phone. It was from Kavita, saying that Krishna ji and Jagmohan ji had left the house. The lady was in a dirty mood. She had a shot and picked up another one to drink. She soon lost her self control and disclosed all her insecurities to Anil.

"I loved him to eternity. I wanted to live with him. I am tired of being strong. I can't fight this world anymore. Tell me, do I have no right to have a peaceful life, a perfect family, and my own children? I don't know whether I was wrong or right in taking that decision at that time, but it has become too taxing for me now. I was fine with the way I have been living, then why has he come back to disturb me again? I have been happy in my space, then what was the need for him to come and create this havoc in my life again. I wish he would have given me a chance to make him understand," she said and started sobbing.

Anil calculated the time. It was the appropriate moment to go and sit next to her. She was feeling betrayed. Carried away due to her drinks, the shattered woman leaned on Anil's shoulder. At the same time, Krishna ji and Jagmohan ji entered the cabin. She kept on saying, "You have such a wonderful family. I too need to be loved, to have a family." She was not aware of her surroundings, as she was quite drunk and not in her senses at all. Anil stood up, stunned and shocked as if a thief had been caught red handed. On one side, he tried to hold and support the semiconscious lady, while on the other, he tried to justify himself to his parents.

"Papa, Mamma...listen." He couldn't let any more words out of his mouth.

Krishna ji felt equally astounded, looking at her son with another lady. Jagmohan ji had to almost pull her out of that cabin.

Chapter 30

The Wedding Twist

How could the senior mother let everyone act so offensively with her? She had planned something for everyone. After that shocking date, the next morning came with a mourning environment at home. A cold war was going on within the family. Everyone was searching for some reason or the other to vent out their feelings. Kavita had a upper hand as what she had assumed had indeed turned out to be the truth, and there was no doubt left anymore about Anil's unfaithfulness towards her. Even the children smelt something fishy going on between the elders of the house. After they left for school, Kavita started the dialogue, "Mamma,Saumya's wedding invitation cards will be reaching us any time now. I am thinking of inviting Subraneel to it. He has been such great help to me in my business. He stays in Mumbai and the wedding is in Mumbai too. If Anil refuses to come, at least Subraneel will be there help me out."

It was a declarative statement for which Krishna ji chose silence to be the best reply. Her expression and body language were enough to.speak of her anger. She stared at Anil. He dropped his gaze in shame, but soon became casual about everything again.

"Mamma, it is not my fault. As a human, I expect some little time to be at ease in this house, but no one has even a single minute to spare for me. in fact, I find it better too stay at my hotel. At least, my staff treats me better as a family."

'Family,' the word rang a bell in Krishna ji's mind. She turned her smile into a smirk and told herself,'I know what kind of family you have at your hotel, and I won't let this go on as long as I am alive. Just wait and watch."

Jagmohan ji had been reading his newspaper quietly. He did not intend to play any music to suit his mood that day. Love has various forms and his newspaper was full of such vices of love. On each page, there were stories of remorse and revenge. He felt peevish and almost threw the newspaper away.

"There are no dignified ways left in this world," he muttered. He was quite annoyed by the situation at home. It was something that nobody had ever expected in their house.

Just then, the door bell rang.

Claccy aunty opened the door. It was a courier delivery man with a box in his hand.

"Mr. Anil's residence?" he enquired.

"H*aan. She spoke. Saab,*" she yelled.

Anil came and collected the courier from him. 'It must be the wedding cards,' he thought. He opened the box. There were a few invitation cards in it. He showed no interest in opening them. Jagmohan ji picked up an invitation card and read it aloud.

Together with their families, Aayush and Saumya invite you to join them in their celebrations at a destination wedding at

'The Fort' Hotels, Goa.

As per programme:

Shagan Ceremony: 4th December

Mehndi ki raat: 5th December

Wedding ceremony: 7th December

Grace the occasion and bless them as they embark upon the journey of a lifetime together.

Instinctively, Anil took the card from his hand and read it again to believe his ears and eyes. At the same time, Kavita approached them to clarify her doubt about the venue too. Krishna ji snickered at the reflex action of her son and daughter-in-law.

This wedding venue was a branch of Anil's hotel itself. When he saw his mother's face, he easily understood who had planned it and how it came to happen. He was filled with admiration for her and wondered how far she could think, just to see the two of them together. Kavita was going through the same emotions too. "Mothers will always be mothers, be it at any age.She cannot leave any stones unturned, specially when it comes to her children." Kavita was touched by that gesture.

'Mamma, I would have come even if the venue had not been changed, but hats off to you,' Anil thought, feeling blessed to have a mother like her; tough as steel, but best in appeal.

Krishna ji had procured all contact numbers from the internet with Tanay's help. Then, she had gone ahead to take Nandita *di* in her confidence. She explained the situation at home to her and made her understand the middle age crisis that her children were going through. She knew that their wanderings would automatically get reduced through a concentrated effort by their loving family, and the wedding twist had definitely been a proof of their love.

There was hardly any time left before the wedding and to convince Rakshanda to attend it was still in the process. Even though Anil had incepted the idea in her mind, things had not quite materialized still. They were actually left with very little time to explore all the avenues. Above all, Subraneel had to go back to Mumbai for a meeting. He flew to Mumbai, without even bidding her goodbye.

She came to office with her eyes still searching for him. Finally, she checked with her staff and got to know about his departure. She took a deep sigh and felt disheartened.

Anil knocked at her door a little while later.

"Come in." She felt better enough to conceal her thoughts this time.Anil entered with the wedding card in his hand, while cribbing nonstop, "It's my mother who purposely planned to shift the wedding venue at the last hour. Can you imagine, it's our own hotel branch in Goa? And the breaking news, Mr. Subraneel came to our house this morning to meet Kavita and she was so happy to welcome him. She invited him to the wedding and he agreed to come too. I feel like an alien in my own house now. I am not going to attend any function. Let them handle it without me. Oh yes! They don't need me now anyway, because Subraneel will be there." His voice was filled with agitation.

He could easily notice Rakshanda turning black and blue. He looked at her and waited for her reaction. She felt like crying but immediately decided that it was not wise to shed tears for someone who could be that mean to her.

The hard core lady started with a piece of advice for Anil. Sounding like a relationship guru, she said, "I think, you are blessed to have such a lovely family. Please don't break your ties with them. I am sure you can win her back with your love and affection. No woman can ever forget the first love of her life and you are her first love. In fact, you must go for the wedding if you ask me. It will help reduce your differences with her."

"No way. I won't attend the wedding as an unwanted guest. She has not asked me even once to come along with her. It's final, I won't go." Mustering up all his frustration, he banged his fist on the table.Rakshanda was speechless. She tried hard to think of some way to convince Anil to go to the wedding, in order to restrict their growing closeness.

Suddenly, she got an idea. "Anil, it is possible for us to go there on work duty from our hotel's side?"

It was the perfect pitch. He bowled her over with his acting skills. Hiding his victorious smile, he raised his brows and creased his forehead before finally approving of the idea.

"It's only because of you, Rakshanda, that I am agreeing to go.However, I will remain just like another employee of the hotel there and not as a guest to that wedding."

Rakshanda felt relieved thinking that she had succeeded in convincing Anil to go to the wedding.How could she possibly know that it had been Anil's plan all along to put those words in

Chapter 31

Get Set Go...Goa

her mouth and get the desired results? But then, all is fair in true love.

The silent war was still on at the house. Anil had booked the tickets to Mumbai for the whole family except for himself. He had also booked two tickets for Aayesha *di* and her son Eeshan, who were coming back to India after a long time. The program was to reach Mumbai by air, from where the event manager had planned a road trip by bus, all the way to Goa.

Anil and Kavita entered their room after dinner.

"Now, what next?" she asked and looked at Anil anxiously.

Anil was equally worried. "This is a critical one. I can handle everything else, but how will I face *di*?"

"You are right. She will arrive tomorrow morning and I am sure she will never accept our apparent differences." Kavita had begun to feel too apprehensive about their drama now. She continued, "If Rakshanda would just accept her love for Subraneel, things would get a lot easier."

"Oh! She definitely loves him, that's why she has planned to come along," Anil smiled.

"Yeah! But now we will have to act out our contempt in front of everyone and it's disturbing me," Kavita said unhappily.

"Don't worry, I think it's quite adventurous to play hide and seek for the love of your life, and meeting after parting is always romantic," Anil said lovingly.

"That's fine, but how will we face *di*?" she asked.

"I don't know, but I'm sure that mamma must be so happy about it. Have you noticed that silence in the house lately?" Anil said nervously.

"I bear it more than you do, dear. It's the silence before the storm. But as far as I know her, she won't say anything to *di* tomorrow, at least, as everyone will be too occupied with last minute packing. The day after is our flight. Let's avoid confronting each other in front of them tomorrow. You are not coming along with us anyway, so we've saved our skin till the time we reach Goa, at least," Kavita suggested.

"I think that's a good idea," Anil said in agreement.

"One more thing, Anil. Please remind me to call Shailesh *jiju* tomorrow. I need to convince him to attend the wedding. It's his all time favourite destination and it will turn out to be a big surprise for *di* too," She told Anil.

Anil smiled and said, "Yes! Your honour."

The next morning, Aayesha's flight arrived before schedule. Anil went to pick them up.

After a long time, the breakfast table enjoyed a chirpy environment again. Krishna ji deliberately withheld the state of affairs at home from Aayesha, as she felt that it was not the appropriate time. However, she observed that both Anil and Kavita were avoiding eye contact with Aayesha. She enjoyed it thoroughly with a faith that there finally was someone there besides herself who could help normalize the situation. She waited for the right time to take Aayesha in her confidence.

Eeshan had come to India after a long time. His Indo-American accent and style impressed Tanay and Tanvi and they all were having a great time together.

The whole day passed by in great hustle and bustle, as everyone had to pack their bags for the wedding. Aayesha *di* got to know about the program but was surprised to know that Anil was not coming along. Anil had not revealed his plans to anyone, so when

Aayesha asked Anil about his program directly, all ears in the house got alert to hear his reply.

"Di, I'll join you at the wedding venue directly. Actually, there is a seminar going on at the hotel here and the wedding venue in Goa is our own hotel branch, so a colleague of mine will also be traveling there with me."

The former part of the answer was expected, but the later part came as a shock to Krishna ji. Her facial expression changed in no time. Since Aayesha had no clue about anything, she took everything normally. Moreover, anything as far fetched as an extramarital affair could not even enter her wildest whims and fancies.

They went out for dinner that night as they had their flight the very next morning. At the end of the day, it felt like a wonderful family reunion after a long time. Everyone loves peace, you see.

Before leaving the house, Kavita felt upset over going alone. She was standing in front of the mirror when Anil approached her from behind. She felt Anil wrap his arms around her waist, reaching up slowly, as he rested his face on her shoulder. "Separation increases the desire to meet again. Wait for me. I'll meet you in Goa." He had read her emotions.

She locked lips with him for a minute and then left. Out of their room, they had to maintain their characters, so there was a silent farewell between them which sent a'something-is-wrong' vibe to Aayesha.

Finally, they boarded their flight and it reached Mumbai as scheduled. A tempo traveler was already waiting for them outside. Everyone was in a ceremonial mood. Amidst all the wedding preparations, no one had the time to ask Kavita anything. Saumya was the only one who knew the truth of their affair, so Kavita was at ease with her. Otherwise, with Nandita *di* or Aayesha *di*, she kept her interaction to a minimum.

She had been sitting with Saumya when her phone pinged. It was obviously Anil. Saumya asked mischievously, "*Masu*?"

She smiled and replied, "Are you not getting any messages from Aayush?"

Saumya blushed and said, "You know *masi*, your love story inspired us so much that whenever we disagree on something, we accept and respect each other's views. If this is love, it's so beautiful, *haina masi*(isn't it)?"

She smiled and asked, "What is their program about the venue?"

"They will come early in the morning on 4th, on the day of the *shagun*. They have booked the same hotel, but the opposite block."

Kavita kissed her on her forehead and blessed her.

Early morning the next day, they left for Goa. It was a wonderful bus journey. Everyone's mood was at an all time high. The event manager had planned it flawlessly. By evening, they reached Goa. They found themselves awestruck by that breath-taking scenery, the disciplined rows of coconut trees standing in attention as if to welcome a chief guest, the mesmerizing view of the valleys, the ever-smiling Goans, the beach side markets and the beautiful sunset. There was something different in the air. Finally, the bus reached its destination,'The Fort'. Needless to say, they received a wonderful welcome. With a refreshing welcome drink, the reception area of the hotel was a real visual treat.

Everyone was thrilled to see that high class 7-star property with three swimming pools and a private beach. It was, undoubtedly, a dream destination.Tea time snacks were about to be arranged, so everyone went to their respective rooms to change. The hotel décor and their well placed amenities won everyone's hearts. The ecstasy of their high spirits made their faces even more vibrant and instead of taking rest, they seemed electro charged in their beach-wears.

"Who wants to sleep in Goa?" the youngsters answered when told to take rest. The reality was that all age groups were actually enjoying the ambience to the best, with tea time gossip over the big family union.

Chapter 32

Ceremonial Vaudeville

Kavita tried to eschew all gossip about her as she was not in a position to be answerable.

The dinner layout was stupendously sumptuous. Finally, Kavita had to confront Aayesha *di.*

"Is everything fine between you and Anil, Kavita?" she came straight to the point.

"It's a long story, *di*. I will tell you in some time," Kavita said, intentionally changing the topic, "When is Shailesh *jiju* coming? I hope he arrives before the functions start."

"Uh! I can't say about him. You know, he is never sure right till the last minute," Aayesha replied.

'Let her have a good sleep tonight. I'll talk to her in the morning," Krishna ji thought while looking at Aayesha.

All the ceremonies were scheduled to start from the next day. The ladies had already scheduled their appointments at the spa, and wanted to catch up on their beauty sleep, while the men, who were some pegs down by this time, just slipped into sleep. The children, on the other hand, were in their own separate world altogether. Kavita found herself wide awake with the thought,'If only Anil were here..." She missed him and closed her eyes to imagine being with him.

The Goan morning sun spread its arms all across the sky and came to peep inside their rooms. Kavita opened her eyes and found Anil sleeping next to her in bed. She had to pinch herself twice to come to terms with the reality.Her smile came back on her face when she kissed him lovingly on his forehead.

She had to get ready for the final set of their drama that day. She knew that Subraneel must have reached the venue by then and if Anil was there, Rakshanda had to be there too. She went out to the coffee lounge where she found Subraneel sitting. They greeted each other with a warm hug. All eyes moved in their direction, and their coffee time ended up becoming a game of Chinese whispers for the family. Rakshanda's ears were not immune to this family gossip either, and she felt very disheartened and out of place by it.

Anil gave proper time for Rakshanda's jealousy meter to reach its peak. He reached the dining hall at breakfast time and brought Rakshanda along with him. He introduced her to everyone else as his colleague. The expression on Krishna ji's face changed as soon as she saw her and Aayesha noticed that immediately. Kavita had also introduced Subraneel to everyone as her business associate. Rakshanda gave her a dense look which could not be evaded. After that, Rakshanda left the place in a bad mood. Things looked very awkward to Aayesha. After breakfast, everyone got busy with preparations for the evening.

Finally, a secret meeting was had between Krishna ji, Nandita *di* and Aayesha *di*.

"IMPOSSIBLE!" Aayesha's eyes bulged out of their sockets in shock when she heard the story.

However, she had to give in to all the valid arguments and evidences against Anil and Kavita. Aayesha correlated these facts to the events that she had witnessed during the morning hours. It was difficult for her to digest, but it seemed true. She called both of them to her to reconfirm what she had got to know.

Anil and Kavita entered her room. There was complete silence for a few seconds. It got on their nerves.

"Are the things spread about you people correct?" As always, *di* did not believe in beating about the bush.

"What, *di*?" Anil pretended to be ignorant.

"I think you know what I am talking about," she spoke angrily, "Even a blind person can notice the differences between you both."

Kavita responded calmly, "Don't worry, *di*. We can pretend otherwise in front of the family."

"Oh! How privileged am I! Go flaunt it, for all I care. You are the parents of two grown teenagers and this is how you behave?Tell me what's on your minds." Her agitation was at its peak.

The door bell rang all of a sudden. Anil opened the door.

"Hello, brother-in-law. What's up?"

Anil was more thrilled than surprised to see Shailesh *jiju* standing right outside the door.

Aayesha found herself with mixed emotions. She couldn't show her agitation to Shailesh, while at the same time, she felt happy about that pleasant surprise from her husband.

'Thanks, *jiju*. You arrived as a life savior today,' Kavita thought to herself.

The best part was that Anil and Kavita could drop their sordid masks for the ceremony and behave like a regular couple after a long time. To be in your own skin is like enjoying your inner freedom. In their natural form, they entered the *Shagun* ceremony.

Saumya was looking extremely pretty and Aayush was being very humble towards everyone. The married men were all set to pull his leg unnecessarily again. Everyone enjoyed the ceremony and all the rituals. Shailesh *jiju* announced for a song to be sung by Anil. Eeshan appealed, "Mamu, no Hindi tonight."

Anil took the mike and started,

"When you are the reason to live

When you are the reason to love

with you every morning seems to be new

I just wanna say, I love you, I love you.

Shed your fears, leave those tears

It's one life to live, let's make it cheers

Cross the hurdles, let's sail through

I just wanna say, I love you,I love you."

While singing the song, he deliberately fixed his gaze at Rakshanda, which made her feel very awkward. Yet, he kept singing,

"Oh! mysterious girl, open up please

Who likes it plain, without any crease

Time is short and the days are few

I just wanna say, I love you, I love you."

It seemed to everyone as if he had been singing for Rakshanda. Kavita and Subraneel kept talking to each other without paying any heed to the situation or to Anil. Rakshanda found it very uncomfortable, so she walked away. The ceremony continued with couple dances and its general liveliness. Saumya and Aayush enjoyed all the rituals and scheduled a pre-wedding photo-shoot for the next day. Aayush wanted to meet Anil without letting anyone know, so he called him up and requested him to come over to a lonely place. Anil went there with Kavita. With Aayush, they could take that risk to be with each other. Aayush requested him to write a nice Punjabi song for his pre wedding photo shoot. There and then, he recited two lines, while holding Kavita's hands,

"Jadon da vekhya main tenu

Kuch vi disda nhi menu,

Loki kende ahi,

Main hosh ich nhi, main hosh ich nhi.

(Since the day I saw you, I can't see anything else. Everyone tells me now that I am lost, I am lost.)

"That's exactly what I want to tell her, *masu*. You are a genius!" Aayush exclaimed.

"Okay, I will give you the whole song before your shoot, alright?" Anil smiled and told him.

After Aayush left, Kavita told him, "It's not happening, dear. It doesn't look like she'll ever speak out her feelings."

"Don't worry, I'll try my last stroke tomorrow." Anil said with determination in his voice.

Chapter 33

The Absolute Countdown

The Goan dance troupe and the guitarist waited at the reception area. They had been called for the ladies sangeet/*mehndi ki raat*. Saumya had just come back from her pre-wedding shoot. She looked vibrant and exuberant, ready to adorn the wedding bliss. She was surrounded by all her friends and relatives. She disclosed the bachelor's night plan arranged for the next day for Ayush from the groom's side. She was a little reluctant due to the common censor attached to a bachelor's night, but since it was already planned, Aayush could not do much about it. She was also little upset with him over the same issue. Kavita read her insecurities and told her to relax, saying ,"Right from the day of your wedding, Aayush will be yours forever." She smiled in response and went to get ready for the mehndi night.

The event was phenomenal. With a Goan dance in Punjabi flavor and the guitarist singing songs on demand, it seemed as if the coconut trees themselves were jiggling to the music. Saumya flaunted her Arabian style mehndi, wearing her sleeveless yellow blouse with a maroon *lehnga* and a turquoise *dupatta*.She also got Aayush's name tattooed in henna on her waist. All the girls seemed very excited about their mehndis. The fun and mirth was on when Anil tried to sneak out of the ceremony.

Rakshanda had not come to attend the ceremony due to a heaviness that she had been feeling. Anil went to her room, unaware that he was being followed by his mother, who had now grown suspicious about everything. He rang the bell and waited for her to open the door. She seemed to be crying. Anil asked her if she would like to join him, as he had been feeling quite lonely too. As she was also undergoing the same feelings, she agreed. Anil escorted her to a swimming pool nearby. There was a dummy yacht built over it, to give a feeling of being on a cruise. The area was dimly lit with some light instrumental music in the background. All of a sudden, Anil proposed to her in the same style as she had been proposed before by Subraneel.

"Nooo," she cried in pain and rushed back to her room.

Anil had given her the biggest shock of her life as his last stroke to bring her lost feelings back. However, it was mistaken by Krishna ji as she came out in person to confront Anil. He was zapped for that moment.

"Oh, no." His mind went blank and his face, expressionless. He had not expected this to happen so he found himself speechless. He tried to escape, but the air between them was silent except for the background music. He could just say, "Mamma, I can't tell you the reason right now, but don't worry, I will sort it out soon."

Krishna ji feared something unusual happening and told her son to maintain decency. Anil promised her to not do anything that could bring shame to her. Then they went back to the Sangeet ceremony.

Aayush had invited the men folk from the bride's side to his stag party too. There were meetings and conspiracies going on. Usually during these wedding scenarios, girls' gang and boys' gang become prominently active. All the men folk were really excited to attend this stag party. Anil told Subraneel to join him at the party. He also asked him to begin the absolute countdown.

Rakshanda had been sitting in her room. The peonies of her thoughts danced with the fragrance of love. She was clear in what she wanted to do. All her blurred thoughts had now reached a clear vision. She had been valiant enough to fight with this male dominated world, but her wandered mind achieved its inner peace only after she won the battle with herself.

Anil knew that she was a hard nut to crack, so had he touched the weakest cord in her in such a manner that the stone-hearted lady had no choice but to meltdown.

A seductively dressed girls' group entered the hotel premises just then. Zealous expressions appeared on the faces of all the men, and the obvious jealous expression on the faces of the ladies. They got really impatient to attend the bachelor's bash. All the young men reached the venue even before time. After all, men will be men and how could they waste even a single moment of this proposed excitement? They eagerly waited for some steamy women to make their appearance and entertain them. But probably their ladies had planned some more surprises for them.

What happened next was something completely unexpected? The women, who were supposed to come erotically dressed, came in wearing Punjabi suits. This doused the fire burning in the hearts of all the gentlemen and the stag party came crashing down right in the beginning.

"Isn't that correct? Don't mess with your girls." These words echoed as a prelude to something coming next.

Then entered their ladies, seductively dressed in off-white dresses with tangerine stilettos. The party really kicked off to a rocking start then. They danced till the party reached its peak. Aayush and Saumya were loving each moment of their togetherness. Kavita was too engrossed in Anil. Aayesha *di* found everything highly confusing. The DJ played all types of dance numbers and no one could stop their feet from tapping. While dancing, dance partners were getting swapped, and at one point, Subraneel found himself dancing with Rakshanda. She was well aware of her emotions at that time and had come to terms with them.

"I love you, Subraneel." Inebriated with love, she slipped in his arms and he caressingly picked her up. As she slipped, the music stopped and everyone looked at them. The world around them seemed to come to a standstill and time stopped at that moment for them. She found herself transfixed in that charm. Lost in that moment, she forgot the world around her. She was with her world, finally. Passionately looking deep into his eyes, she expressed her emotions:

Dhal rhi hai sham, bhar le bahon ke ghere mein mujhe

Aaj taqdeer ne humpe farmaya hai karam , insha allah,insha allah

Pee le ye husne jam, ki abhi hasin hai sham

Vaar denge khud ko hi aaj tujhpe sanam, insha allah, insha allah.

(Before the night unveils, before the dawn prevails

Enrich me with your charms, embrace me in your arms

Today, the luck is on our side, let's celebrate love with pride)

Subraneel kissed her on her forehead and stepped out, while carrying her in his arms and lovingly looking into her eyes. At long last, he had met his world too.

The suspense was finally relieved like the unfurling leaves of a lotus flower. Aayesha *di* looked at Anil and Kavita with sisterly affection and Anil told her to keep it a secret for just one more day.

The Goan sun raised its arms with its orangish red bloom the next morning and peeped out from behind the coconut trees. The kiss of the sun left the sky blushing. The morning was as calm as a sleeping child. All the thunders had now come to rest in peace and the longing for freedom had evaporated. Love is the basis of all existence in this world and when life seems beautiful, it is due to the love in your life. Undoubtedly, love was spreading its wings everywhere.

Krishna ji shared her insecurities with Nandita and Aayesha by telling them about what she had witnessed on the night of *mehendi*. Aayesha pretended to be worried, as she had promised Anil that she would't reveal anything about their secret affair before time.

Amidst all the excitement and exhilaration, the wedding ceremony took place at the sea shore. When everyone reached the wedding venue, they saw two decorated *mandaps* there. It was a big surprise for them. Krishna ji feared the unknown again and told Aayesha to call Anil immediately, but neither Anil, nor Kavita was to be found. In sometime, Saumya, along with Rakshanda, came out in their bridal attires along with Kavita. Behind them, the two grooms entered with their complete entourage. Anil was also with them. A small stage was set up, where a live comedy performance was planned for later. Subraneel went on stage, took the mike in his hands and proposed to her, "Rakshanda, I love you. Will you marry me?"

She blushed and nodded her head in a 'yes'.

Everyone clapped. Krishna ji, Jagmohan ji, Tanay and Tanvi looked at each other in utter surprise.

Subraneel was still at the mike. He expressed his gratitude to Anil and Kavita for having made him realize the true meaning of love. Then, he handed the mike over to Anil.

Anil took his position on stage with the mike and swept his gaze over the gathering. Then he kept his views on love:

"My dear people of all generations, kids, teens, the youth, parents, and grandparents,

Love is the basic necessity for any living being. It makes a person valuable. At any age, love comes with its own hue.So today, I request you all to feel free with the love of your life and say it in front of your children, in front of your parents. Papa, Mamma, we are really sorry if we hurt your sentiments, but in between the demands of our children and the commands of our parents, we got so lost that we ended up planning to mingle secretively and so the jingle continues."

All the bits and pieces of the story were then joined to make sense and everyone laughed heartily.

"You are right. We could not understand our responsibility to give you your space. But now, you get ready to face the punishment for having tortured us so," Krishna ji spoke affectionately and then called Tanay and Tanvi towards her. The awesome foursome then handed over a packet to Anil and Kavita, while yelling, "Surprise!"

Jagmohan ji said in a jest, "We thought we would surprise you, but yours' was a far better one."

They laughed, as Anil opened the packet.

"A couple's trip to Paris!"

"Wow! Mamma, you knew about us." Kavita asked, still in doubt.

"Well! This time, you actually managed to steal my mental peace and I could not have imagined the truth even in my wildest dreams. To remind you two of your love for each other, we planned this trip. However, now it shall be to celebrate your love, my dear." Krishna ji admitted that she had been fooled, but she was happy about it.

"I thought you might have linked my Ahmadabad trip with her Mumbai trip drama," Anil smiled.

"If only I could. I guess my age has taken over my ability to think cleverly, and you were really unfair to me too," Krishna ji remarked.

"Mamma," said Kavita, "Let's celebrate love together and I know our dear both generations will give us our WE TIME too. We will all go to Paris together."

The night tides danced in the moonlit night and the star studded sky showered its blessings on the newly wedded as well as the formerly wedded couples.